HIGH HURDLES

Moving Up

HIGH HURDLES

Moving Up

LAURAINE SNELLING

BETHANY HOUSE PUBLISHERS
MINNEAPOLIS, MINNESOTA 55438

Published by Bethany House Publishers
11400 Hampshire Avenue South
Bloomington, Minnesota 55438
www.bethanyhouse.com

Bethany House Publishers is a Division of
Baker Book House Company, Grand Rapids, Michigan.

Printed in the United States of America

Library of Congress Cataloging-in-Publication Data

Snelling, Lauraine.
    Moving up / by Lauraine Snelling.
        p. cm. — (High hurdles ; 7)
    Summary: Now that the new house is completed, DJ realizes she's
about to leave the only home she's ever known, and she's not ready to
say goodbye.
ISBN 0–7642–2035–7 (pbk.)
    [1. Moving, Household—Fiction. 2. Horses—Fiction.
3. Stepfamilies—Fiction. 4. Christian life—Fiction.] I. Title.
II. Series: Snelling, Lauraine. High hurdles ; bk. 7.
PZ7.S677   Mo   1998
[Fic]—dc21   00267156
                                             CIP
                                             AC

To Ruby and Pat—
You've been with me from the beginning.
Thanks for helping make my life fuller,
richer, and more fun.

LAURAINE SNELLING fell in love with horses by age five and never outgrew it. Her first pony, Polly, deserves a book of her own. Then there was Silver, Kit—who could easily have won the award for being the most ornery horse alive—a filly named Lisa, and an asthmatic registered Quarter Horse called Rowdy, and Cimeron, who belonged to Lauraine's daughter, Marie. It is Cimeron who stars in *Tragedy on the Toutle*, Lauraine's first horse novel. All of the horses were characters, and all have joined the legions of horses who now live only in memory.

While there are no horses in Lauraine's life at the moment, she finds horses to hug in her research, and she dreams, like many of you, of owning one or three again. Perhaps a Percheron, a Peruvian Paso, a . . . well, you get the picture.

Lauraine lives in California with her husband, Wayne, basset hound, Woofer, and cockatiel, Bidley. Her two sons are grown and have dogs of their own; Lauraine and Wayne often dog-sit for their golden retriever granddogs. Besides writing, reading is one of her favorite pastimes.

1

"NEW YORK! YOU WANT ME to go to New York?"

Gran and Joe both nodded.

"Me, Darla Jean Randall? At only fourteen, I can go to New York City and see Madison Square Garden, where Major and I will jump someday and—"

"It's not much to see." Joe Crowder, whom DJ had dubbed GJ for Grandpa Joe, crossed his arms across the broad chest that used to wear the badge of the San Francisco Mounted Police. Until he retired and married DJ's grandmother, that is. "All you see is an ugly marquee on a dirty street right off Times Square."

DJ, as Darla Jean demanded everyone call her, finger combed her sun-streaked blond hair up from the sides and to the top of her head. Green eyes sparkled in delight as she looked from one grandparent to the other and back again. "Times Square. Where that big ball drops on New Year's Eve?"

"Yep, that very spot."

DJ wrapped her arms around herself and hugged her shoulders. Spinning in place, she crooned, "I'm going to New York. I'm going to New York." The spin stopped with her facing Gran. Taller by four inches, she looked down at her grandmother. "When? When do we go?"

7

"Well, first of all, you have to ask your mother and father."

"Oh . . . right." It was still hard to remember that she now had a dad who lived in the same house she did. "And?"

"And we go the second weekend in April."

"April! N-o-o-o." DJ's chin hit her chest, and her shoulders melted. "Why does everything fun have to happen at the same time?"

"Now what?" Joe shifted to draw DJ close with one arm.

"That's the weekend of the art classes in San Francisco with Isabella Gant." She gave her grandmother a hopeful glance. "No chance you could change the date?"

"Hardly, darlin'. The date of the award ceremony is set long in advance." Gran was being honored for her illustrations in the field of children's literature, and DJ had helped with the drawings of a foal in the book that was receiving the award.

"I knew that. I was just hoping." She looked at Gran through her long eyelashes. "I could skip—"

"Don't even go there. You are *not* missing out on that. I have a feeling that studying drawing with Isabella Gant will be a life-changing experience for you."

"She can't be a better teacher than you are."

"Ah, Darla Jean, you are the light of my life." Gran wrapped her arms around DJ's waist—the one DJ often insisted she didn't have. Straight poles don't have waists.

"Don't worry, kid. You'll be jumping at Madison Square Garden soon enough, and then we'll do the town." Joe pushed away from the counter and crossed to the refrigerator. "Got anything to eat in here?" He stuck his head inside the just opened door.

"There are carrots and celery in the drawer, all fixed."

"More rabbit food?" He groaned. "How about a chunk of cheese or a—"

"Joe Crowder, you know what the doctor said."

Joe muttered something unintelligible.

"And if you are sneaking something else, you just get out of there."

He backed out in time to avoid getting smacked by the door Gran had given a hard nudge. "Not fair." He checked inside the refrigerator again.

DJ and Gran swapped "good grief" looks.

"Come on, GJ, let's go take care of the horses." DJ turned to Gran. "Don't feel bad about the trip—my mother probably wouldn't have let me go anyway. She doesn't like her daughter to have too much fun."

Joe snapped upright, slamming the fridge door. "Not her fault you let your grades fall—and don't be a smart mouth. It doesn't sound or look good on you."

DJ at least had the grace to look ashamed. "Sorry." *But it's true*, she thought. *My mother is more interested in the twins than me most of the time. And she's rabid about my grades. All because of that stupid algebra.* And now Joe was on her case, too. She hunched her shoulders. Why couldn't she learn to keep her mouth shut?

Waving good-bye to Gran, she followed Joe out to the forest green Explorer.

"So what brought that up?" Joe turned the ignition, and the Explorer's engine roared to life.

"What?" DJ assumed her most innocent expression.

"Don't give me that." The sound of his voice more than his words told her he'd kicked into policeman mode. And as he'd often said, he'd been a master interrogator during his days with the force.

And still was.

"I don't know."

"Sure you do—just think about it. You and your mother must have gotten into it again."

"Come on, Joe. When don't we?"

"And you'd never exaggerate, either, would you?" He flipped the turn signal.

"Me? Never."

He turned into the driveway of Briones Riding Academy, where they both stabled their horses and DJ taught beginning riding, trained a rowdy gelding, and took lessons in both jumping and dressage.

When she started to open the door, Joe stopped her with a hand on her arm. "Isn't the algebra coaching with Robert helping any?"

"Not much." DJ looked up at him, shaking her head. "How come I'm so dumb in math when I can get pretty good grades in about everything else?"

"You're not dumb. And I don't ever want to hear you say so again. But some people do seem to have a block in some areas. You are good with words and are an incredible artist—that comes from the creative side of the brain, the right side. Math comes from the left side, the analytical side, and that's not where your strengths lie. But sticking with the math will help develop that area."

"GJ, I even pray about the problems before I do them, but God doesn't seem to be listening—or else He doesn't care if I do algebra, either."

DJ's fingernails screamed to be chewed. She tucked them under her thighs for safekeeping.

"Oh, He cares all right. What lessons do you suppose He is trying to teach you?"

DJ wrinkled her nose. "Can I think about that? I gotta get Patches on the hot walker."

"Sure 'nuff." He removed the keys from the ignition. "I'll groom Major for you. Ranger can wait his turn." Ranger was the Quarter Horse gelding Joe had bought with the dream of someday entering cutting competitions.

"Thanks." DJ bailed from the sport utility vehicle as if bloodhounds were after her. That man could drive her nuts with his questions. Did he always have to be right?

She stopped in the office long enough to check the duty board, even though she knew exactly what she had to do. Sure enough, Amy was cleaning stalls on the south aisle of the low red barn. They hadn't ridden home from school together since Amy had been to the orthodontist to get her braces tightened. But DJ knew if she stopped to talk with Amy now, she wouldn't get to see Major until all her work was done.

She opted for Major. As soon as he heard her voice, he nickered. When she didn't answer, he whinnied.

"What a welcome!" DJ plugged her ears as she jogged toward him. Another horse whinnied, then others. Whinnying was as catching as a yawn.

"You big goof, what's with you?" She hid both hands behind her back. When he nudged an arm, she palmed the carrot for him. "Had to work for it, didn'tcha?" He nosed her other arm and got half a horse cookie.

DJ wrapped both arms around his neck and squeezed, earning slobber in her ear for the effort.

"You are the very, very, very best horse any girl could ever own."

He flicked his ears back and forth and whiskered her cheek, bathing her in carrot- and molasses-laden horse breath.

She scratched the spot between his ears that he especially liked, then gave him a pat on the nose and stepped away. "Back in a while. Got to get to work."

He nickered as she left, making her want to stay with him even more. If only she could ride him. Would her mother *never* let her off restrictions? And all because of two lousy *C*s on her report card, one a C minus in algebra.

While Patches, the young gelding she trained for Mrs. Johnson, kept the hot walker squealing in protest at his fits and starts, DJ gathered his tack and took it back to his stall.

She tossed out some newly dirtied shavings and dug a hoof-pick out of the grooming bucket. Patches nickered when she came for him, tossing his head and striking out with one front hoof.

"Oh great. Who poured extra energy in *your* feed?"

He nickered again and nuzzled her pockets when she got close enough. She pushed his nose away and unhooked the lead shank from the hot walker. Snapping her own lead in place, she led him back to the barn.

"Knock it off," she ordered when he bumped her with his shoulder the second time. She jerked on his lead shank and planted her feet. "Now, listen here, pea brain, you are not going to act up today. You are going to behave yourself, you hear?"

Patches wore his "who me?" look. He shook his head, then all over, his mane flying as if a wind had blown through. He snorted again, rubbed his forehead on her shoulder, and blew.

"Are you finished?" She had a hard time keeping from laughing. "You are such a ham."

She kept up a running commentary while she groomed him and picked his hooves. He didn't even puff up his belly when she cinched the saddle. "Uh-oh, don't tell me you gave up on being a brat."

Patches behaved for the entire lesson.

"You know, if you acted like this for your owner, she wouldn't be walking around with a broken arm."

"And *she* would be riding instead of you." Bridget Sommersby, owner of Briones Riding Academy and DJ's coach and friend, leaned on the aluminum fence that wrapped around the covered arena.

DJ rode over to the rail. "He looks good, doesn't he?"

"He does, thanks to you. But I do agree with what you have been telling me. He is too much horse for Mrs. Johnson. She needs an animal she can have fun riding, not have to watch every minute. Thank God she was not seriously injured the other day."

"I hate to see him go." DJ patted Patches' neck. "Maybe if I'd—"

"Do not finish what you are thinking. You have done all you can with this guy." Bridget stroked Patches' nose. "Given six more months with you, he might settle down, but he might need a couple more years, too. In all honesty, we cannot take that chance."

"Do you know of a good horse that might suit her?"

"No, but I am sure we will find one. Andrew does not need all this stress, either." Andrew was Mrs. Johnson's eight-year-old son, who was working hard to overcome his fear of horses. His mother's accident had sent him into a panic.

Bridget looked up at DJ. "And you, *ma petite*, are not to blame yourself in any way for this not working out. You did your best, and your best was very good. Do you hear me?"

DJ bit her bottom lip and nodded. A compliment like that from Bridget was rare enough to make it shine like gold in the sun. And the order was unmistakable. She bit back the *but* and nodded again. "Thank you."

"We will talk with her together." Bridget started to turn away and looked over her shoulder. "How long until you are off restrictions?"

"I don't know. Mom said until my grades come up, and I flunked the last algebra test."

"That is not good." Bridget stroked her forefinger along her jawbone. "And you are working with a tutor?"

DJ nodded. "My fa—" She stumbled over the word *father*. "Robert. But we just started."

"You can accomplish this." Bridget held up a hand. DJ knew it meant no excuses. Bridget didn't tolerate excuses. "Anyone as stubborn as you can do anything she sets her mind to."

DJ hugged those words to her heart as she put Patches away. Her new father had said the same thing.

But what if you can't? a little voice inside her head sneered. *You might never ride Major again. And then you might just as well forget about the Olympics.*

2

"I'M AFRAID I HAVE SOME BAD NEWS." Robert Crowder looked around at his family gathered at the dinner table that evening.

"What is that, dear?" Lindy continued cutting up pork chops for the five-year-old twins, Bobby and Billy.

"It looks like moving day is delayed—again."

The boys groaned, making a big deal out of it as usual.

In DJ's opinion, they did nothing quietly, even sleep. She looked up at Robert. "What happened?"

"The inspector found some problems with the garage door. . . ."

"So? We don't live in the garage." The words popped out before she had time to think.

Bobby—or was it Billy?—giggled beside her. DJ groaned along with the two boys, one on either side of her. The only time she could tell Bobby and Billy apart was when one wore a bandage. She was tempted to apply one with super-bond, forever-permanent glue.

"I sure wish it were that simple. But there's more."

DJ studied his face across the table. Robert looked tired, not sleepy but worn out. Bags under his blue eyes were not the norm, nor was the gray color of his skin.

Lindy handed the boys their plates and turned to her

15

husband. "You said there's more."

He nodded. "Ummm. Maria can't come out yet. The doctor says she needs more rest before coming back to work." Maria Ramos had cared for the twins as nanny since their mother died two years earlier. A bad case of pneumonia had struck while Lindy and Robert were on their honeymoon, and Maria still hadn't fully recovered.

Now it was Lindy's turn to groan. "And I have to leave for that conference in Chicago day after tomorrow. I can't put that off. It wouldn't be so bad, but Mother and Joe are going to Los Angeles the same day, so they can't help out, either. What are we going to do?" She rubbed her forehead with her fingertips. "I was counting on Maria's coming back."

Robert sighed. "I know. But we'll figure out something."

DJ concentrated on her food. *Please don't ask me to watch the boys after school. I have to work, too.*

"Let's discuss it later. DJ, how was school?"

She shrugged. She figured he meant algebra since he'd started coaching her a few days before. Might as well get the bad news over quick. "I flunked the test."

"What is flunked?" the twin on her right asked.

"Is it bad?" asked the other.

She couldn't bring herself to look Robert in the face. "Sorry."

"That means we'll just have to work harder." He shook his head when she looked up at him. "No, don't even think it. There is no way you are getting out of algebra, and you are not having trouble because you are stupid or dumb. I've been giving this some thought, and I believe your teacher just hasn't explained things in a way you understand."

"Ain't that the truth," DJ muttered under her breath.

"Darla Jean." The warning came from her mother. Use of her full name meant DJ had better keep her mouth shut. If only she could shut off her mind as easily.

"Do you ask questions in class?" Robert wiped his mouth with his napkin.

DJ shook her head.

"Why not?"

It was DJ's turn to sigh. "I don't know. I guess by the time I've got a question other than 'huh?' figured out, he's on to something else and I feel like an idiot for being so slow."

"Okay." Robert nodded and spoke at the same time. "How about if we have a parent/teacher/pupil conference? See if we can get some help."

DJ felt like saying "Oh goody," but this time she wisely kept her comment to herself. The little voice in her head reminded her, *I thought you said you were going to whup algebra? You better show some enthusiasm here.*

"Daddy, so when we gonna move?"

"We wants a pony."

Saved by the twins. Sometimes they did come in handy.

The discussion switched to furniture being lost somewhere in Kansas; DJ wondered if the twister that took Dorothy to the Land of Oz had snatched their new furniture. She zoned out, and in her mind she took Major over the jumps, a perfect round with an audience applauding and cheering her on.

"DJ!" She came back to the present with a thump. The voice calling her name certainly wasn't coming from a loudspeaker.

"Huh?"

"I asked you a question." Her mother's voice dripped icicles.

DJ looked up at her mother. "Sorry." A glance at Robert's face showed him studying her. One eyebrow raised when he caught her glancing at him.

"Mommy, I gotta go potty." The twin on the right squirmed in his chair. The other followed suit.

"You boys can be excused. Remember to wash your hands before you come back to the table. We have devotions, so don't waste time in the bathroom." Robert turned from them to look at DJ again.

She now knew what a bug under a microscope felt like.

He tented his fingers and rested his chin on them. "DJ, where were you just now?"

"Right here." But she knew what he meant. Where had she been in her head? She stammered when he continued his scrutiny. "I . . . I was thinking about jumping Major."

Lindy huffed and rolled her eyes.

A familiar slow burn in her middle caught DJ's attention. A fight was coming on—she could taste it.

"Do you do that often?" One finger tapped on his chin. "Come on, honesty here. We have no time for playing games."

DJ tried to think. *Often? What counts as often?* "Sometimes."

"During algebra?"

DJ could feel the heat creeping up from her neck to her face. She nodded. Oh, if only she could chew her fingernails. But ever since she'd started applying her *I can do all things through Christ who strengthens me* verse, she'd learned to sit on her fingers to keep from chewing. Her nails looked good now, except of course when she snagged one at the barn. But sometimes she *needed* to chew her nails. Like right now.

"I can see the wheels turning in your head. Care to share what's happening?"

The bug under the microscope squirmed in her seat. She let out a sigh so heavy her chair squeaked in protest. "I was thinking how bad I need to chew on a fingernail."

Robert burst out laughing.

DJ stared at him. This was no laughing matter. She

checked. Did he hurt her feelings? Nope. But when you think of it . . .

She tried to keep the grin from tickling her cheeks, but when he continued to laugh, she joined in. Lindy looked from one to the other, shaking her head all the while.

"You two are certifiably nuts." But she smiled as she said it.

When the boys came back in the room, they looked at the three at the table and shrugged in unison, a trick they had with everything, and climbed up on their chairs.

"Devotions . . ."

"Daddy." One began the sentence, the other finished it.

The verse Robert read fit right in. " 'The joy of the Lord is my strength.' " When he asked, "Can you have joy when you are sad?" the boys shook their heads.

"Trick question, right?"

Robert winked at her. "Right, DJ. Joy has nothing to do with how happy or sad you are. Joy is a gift from God, not a feeling like the others." He looked at the twins. "Who brings us joy?"

They spoke at the same time. "Jesus."

Like them, DJ had long ago figured out that seventy-five percent of the questions asked by pastors and Sunday school teachers could be answered by the word *Jesus*. A song from her younger days trickled into her mind. "I've got the joy, joy, joy, joy down in my heart. . . ." The tune wouldn't go away as she tried to listen to what Robert had to say.

"Good answer, guys." Lindy smiled at them both.

A bit later when they bowed their heads in prayer, DJ squeezed the hands on either side of her. She did have joy in her heart, and right now she wanted to share it with her family.

But trying to keep the joy intact while she struggled with an algebra problem wasn't easy. Her algebra book in tow, DJ and Robert returned to the dining room table after it was cleared. It wasn't long before DJ began shaking her head.

"I don't get it."

"I know."

"How do you know?"

"DJ, your face is like an open book with big print, not hard to read at all. But keep in mind, I can also see when you check out. And I have a feeling that is part of your problem."

"I didn't realize I did that." She closed her math book and put her papers back in her notebook.

"Well, understanding or being aware of something is the first step to change. I'll be praying that you can keep your mind on what the teacher is saying and on the work itself." He looked deep into her eyes. "I believe you can do algebra, Darla Jean Randall. I believe that with the grace of God, you can do anything you set out to do."

She swallowed at the sound of his voice and the caring she read on his face.

"I won't let you down." The whispered promise came unbidden.

"You won't let yourself down then, either. Algebra is no different from learning to jump, once you make the commitment."

She cocked an eyebrow at him. "Don't think I'd go *that* far." But she knew what he meant.

He laid a hand on her arm. "Now, what don't you understand about this lesson tonight?"

DJ thought a minute. "I don't know, I think I got it." She repeated back to him the material they'd covered.

"Good for you." The smile he gave her was almost as good as a compliment from Bridget.

The next day in class, she caught her mind wandering off when Mr. Henderson was talking. She jerked it back and focused on the front of the room. She watched carefully as he did one of the equations on the board.

"Now, are there any questions?" He turned and faced the class again.

DJ raised her hand. "Could you go over that one more time, please?"

"Sure will." As he did, DJ realized it sorta made sense.

"You got it now?" The teacher looked right at her and waited.

She could feel her heart hammer as some of the other kids turned to look at her, too. She wrinkled her forehead, struggling to get it right.

Mr. Henderson nodded. "Let me go over it again." He turned back to the board and redid the equation, saying much the same thing again but slowly and clearly.

DJ muttered to herself along with him. *So if 2x plus 3y equals 60, and 2x plus 5 equals 35, then x equals 15 and y equals 10.*

She nearly jumped out of her seat to run around the room, shouting for joy. It made sense! She got it for a change.

When she walked up to her locker after class, Amy turned to look at her. "You look jazzed. What's up?"

"Mr. Henderson and algebra. I think I got it!"

"A miracle has happened!"

Several students turned their way at Amy's shout but DJ didn't care. She felt like shouting, too. She did just that when Joe picked them up after school.

"Wait till I tell Robert." She dropped her backpack on the floor and turned to Joe. "I even asked Mr. Henderson to go over it one more time. And he did!" She shook her head and flopped against the back of the seat. "I'm hungry."

"I think this deserves a hot fudge sundae. What do you think, Amy?"

"Yes!"

"What's Gran going to say?" DJ asked as she, Joe, and Amy climbed back in the truck after their stop. She licked the last smidgen of fudge off her lips. "About your diet, I mean."

"Plenty. But it'll be worth every word. And when I tell her why we celebrated, she'll ask why we didn't take her along."

Back at the barns, chores went quickly, but leaving Major again without riding him made DJ hurt inside. He nickered after her, tossing his head as if pleading for a workout.

"What's up?" Joe asked when she climbed into the truck.

"Major's going soft. Fourteen days since I rode him. He'll forget everything we've been working on." She slumped and crossed her arms over her chest. "If only I knew how long this . . ." The word she felt like saying would have earned her a scolding if not worse, so she wisely cut it off. "This restriction"—she made it sound like a dirty word—"is going to last."

"So there. What happened to the good mood?"

"Joe, this isn't funny. I've got to ride Major."

"So when's your next algebra test?"

She shrugged. "Who knows? My teacher springs pop quizzes without warning."

"About how often?"

"Too often." She slanted him a look from the corner of her eye. "Funny, right now I'm looking forward to a quiz. If that don't beat all."

Joe set the Explorer in motion and let the silence be. They were about to DJ's driveway when she spoke up. "What if I screw up again?" Her voice sounded like a little girl's.

"Then you back up, relearn, review, and give it another shot. Ninety percent of success in anything is confidence. If you had it once, you'll get it again. Just don't go around expecting perfection the first time out."

"Easy for you to say. No one puts you on restrictions."

"Oh, not now. But the stories I could tell you . . ."

Her interest perked up. "Like what?"

"Like you better get in the house so you're not late. I know Robert is going to be pleased with your news." He rested his wrists on the top of the steering wheel. "Hey, how about if I feed the horses in the morning and you take the afternoon. Your grandmother and I are going to Los Angeles for a couple of days."

"Okay."

"I'll ride Major, too, so he gets some exercise."

"Thanks, GJ. See ya tomorrow." DJ bailed from the truck and trotted up to the house.

"Hurry, DJ, we's hungry." The twins met her at the door. "Where's Mom?"

"Working. Daddy and us made dinner."

"Oh." DJ took the stairs two at a time, the boys following her. "You guys wait down there, okay? Maybe you can set the table or something."

"Hurry."

"Guess what?" DJ slid onto her chair.

Robert looked up from setting a casserole dish in the center of the table. "What?"

"I asked Mr. Henderson to do a problem over."

"And?"

"And I got it. The thing made sense."

"All right, DJ!" He gave her a thumbs up. "Way to go."

Once grace was said and the plates were filled, Robert looked across the table at DJ. "I hate to ask this after your good news, but is there any way you can watch the boys after school tomorrow? I know you don't teach on Friday and . . ." He shrugged. "Basically, I don't know what else to do. I have to be in San Mateo for a meeting."

There she went, feeling like that bug under the microscope again. Who would feed the horses? And what about Patches?

3

I SHOULD HAVE JUST SAID NO.
You can't. He's your father now.
But how can I work all this out?
The thoughts waged war in her mind. DJ lay back on her bed, one leg crossed over the other. She felt like beating on the bed with her heels. Now she couldn't even go over to the barn, let alone ride. And all because of those two stu— She shut off that line of thought. It wasn't the twins' fault.

"Fiddle! Double and triple fiddle!" She glared at the spot on the ceiling that looked like the monster in *Beauty and the Beast* when she squinted her eyes just right. And on top of all that, Robert didn't have time to help her with algebra tonight.

"DJ?" The twins spoke as one.

"Go away."

"DeeJaaay!" This time they tapped on her door.

"Go ask your dad." Emphasis on *dad*. Right now she didn't want to even hear his name.

"He's busy."

"On the phone."

And I'm not? I've got homework up to my eyebrows and two bratty boys bugging me. She rolled off her bed and to her feet, all in one smooth motion. Jerking the door open, she hissed, "Go watch a video."

Two lower lips quivered and tears pooled in their eyes faster than she could blink.

"You heard me, now go." She made shooing motions with her hands.

One tear rolled over a rounded cheek. They stared up at her, waiting for her to change her mind.

DJ steeled herself against the tear.

Another trickled down, on the other face.

"Look, I've got homework to do. Go get a book and read."

"Can't read—" sniff—"yet."

"Then look at the pages." DJ shut the door in their faces and leaned against it. When she heard them shuffle down the hall, she sat at her desk. Now she felt lower than dirt. She propped her head up in her hands. One little voice whispered, *Call them back.* The other said, *Good going, girl. That told them.*

When she closed her eyes, she could see Gran's sorrowful face.

DJ sucked in a deep breath. She'd read to them later. Right now—she slammed open her history book and began reading. Taking notes as she read was the only way she could keep her mind on her homework. Two pairs of swimming blue eyes kept intruding.

When she got to the algebra, she stopped cold. Getting up and going to the window, she peered out. Rain. Oh great. It looked about as happy as she felt.

How come everyone left everything up to her? A few days ago they said they'd help her, and here she was getting saddled with the twins after school. What kind of help was that? And Robert promised to help her with algebra and he bailed out.

Just like you flunked out with the boys.

"But I didn't promise to read to them every night." She made a face at the reflection in the window. Back to her desk. She sank into the chair and stared at the wall. A card caught her eye. *"I can do all things through Christ who strengthens me."*

"I bet whoever wrote that didn't have to do algebra."

You said you'd not just try but do your best.

She whirled away from the chair and paced the room. If only there was some way to shut off smart small voices.

"Darla Jean Randall, I am totally ashamed of you."

DJ spun around as her mother's tap at the door preceded her entry by only a millisecond.

"Now what'd I do?" She saw the boys, cheeks tear streaked, standing behind her mother.

DJ groaned.

"It's not what you did but what you didn't!" Lindy planted her hands on her hips. "As a member of this family, you can accept some responsibility around here."

"I'm trying to. I have a mountain of homework, and I'm trying to get it done so I can bring my grades up, like you demanded." White-hot anger surged clear up from her toes.

"Your brothers needed you."

"Isn't it enough that I have to watch them tomorrow? I can't do it all!"

Lindy clamped her teeth so hard that her jaw turned white. "We will discuss this later." Lindy spun on her heel and stalked out the door, closing it behind her with a very decided click.

DJ could hear her murmuring to the boys, her tone all sweetness now.

"Not fair! She's not fair at all!" DJ stomped around the room. When she passed her desk, she swept the algebra book to the floor and kept on pacing.

"Little sneaks. Got to have their own way all the time.

And she buys right into it. Spoiled brats, that's what they are." The more she muttered, the more she paced, the hotter she burned. Instead of tears, steam formed in her eyes. At least, that's what it felt like. Hot and burning. She blew her nose, and with that, the tears broke loose and ran down her face.

She dashed them away and continued pacing. Why was everything always her fault? Now she'd probably be on restrictions clear into eternity.

She slumped on the edge of the bed. "Boy, Randall, when you wipe out, you do it with a bang."

Back at her desk, she looked again at the Bible verse. "God, if I'm supposed to be able to do all things, how about some extra hours in the day?" She stared at the open pages of her textbook. "And a brain that gets this stuff easy so I don't have to waste so much time on it?"

She turned back to the day's lesson, the one she finally understood. As she reread it, she could remember what it meant. So the next lesson would only carry things one step further. She muttered the equation over and over as she worked to finish the assignment. She managed all but the story problem at the end.

And who could she tell? Her mother hated her—or close to it. Robert was still on the phone for all she knew. The boys wouldn't understand, and Amy couldn't talk on the phone after nine. After a moment of thought, she glanced toward the ceiling. "You want to say 'I told you so'?" She snorted. "I can say thank you, though. I got the assignment done all by myself." She thought a moment. "No, I got my assignment done with *your* help, right? So thanks a whole bunch. Now, if you could do something about my mother . . ."

Even after she'd gotten into her Snoopy nightshirt and brushed her teeth, there was no sign of her mother. DJ stuffed her books and papers into her backpack and set it on the chair, ready for the morning. She looked through her closet and decided what to wear. Padding down the hall to the bathroom again, she could tell the boys were sleeping. Only the night-light in their room showed through the cracked-open door. Light still shone under her mother's door. The downstairs was dark.

"So is Mom coming or not?" she asked the face in the mirror.

No answer, so after flushing the toilet, she headed back to her room. What a perfect ending to a perfect day. "Ha!"

With the lights out and DJ snuggled down under the covers, she could no longer ignore the voice. Right, she'd lost her temper again. Right, she'd been mean to the twins. Right, she was about as good as a load of dirty shavings being carted out of the barn.

"God, I'm sorry. Please forgive me?" But she knew she needed to ask her mother's forgiveness. Robert probably hated her, too. And if she didn't get to ride soon, Major would hate her.

"Where's Mom?" she asked in the morning. Robert had the phone clutched between shoulder and ear as he poured milk over the boys' cereal.

"Already gone to the airport." He turned back to the phone. "I told you there is no way we can manage that."

DJ got a food bar out of the drawer and poured herself a glass of milk. Chugalugging that, she slipped out the door at the first honk of the Yamamoto car horn.

"You'll be here for the boys?" Robert called out the door as she started to get in the car.

"Yes!" She dumped her backpack on the floor and slumped into the seat, snapping her seat belt in place.

"Boy, if you don't look happy." Amy tucked a strand of

dark straight hair behind her ear.

"Don't ask."

"I won't."

"I have to baby-sit the twins after school. Joe is gone, so I'm taking care of Ranger, too. Any chance you could feed the horses for me tonight?"

"Remember, we're going to Grandma's. You won't be going to the Academy today." Mrs. Yamamoto looked over the seat. "Sorry, DJ, but it's my mother's birthday. Amy will be leaving school early."

"Who's feeding Josh?" Josh was Amy's half Arab gelding. They rode and showed Western.

"I was going to ask you." Amy leaned back against the seat.

"I can't believe this. Who are we supposed to ask? Bridget?"

"That'll be the day. How are you getting home from school?"

DJ slapped the heel of her hand against her forehead. "You'd think someone would wonder about that. They just took it for granted that I could ride with you, I guess." *Or rather, no one gave you a thought*, the little voice whispered. *"Good old dependable DJ. She's supposed to be a miracle worker."*

Mrs. Yamamoto looked at her in the rearview mirror. "If you can get an excuse to leave school early, I could drop you off on our way to the birthday party."

DJ nodded. "Thanks, I'll talk to Ms. Benson."

By the time she explained the whole mess to the vice-principal, the bell rang so DJ was late for first period. "It would have been easier to just skip," she muttered as she jogged down the hall to her classroom. "Besides, this is Good Friday. Should've had today off anyway." But the pink slip to excuse her now resided in her back pocket. Ms. Benson had said she didn't do this for many students. But she knew DJ never skipped or lied, so she could trust her.

When DJ got home, the message on the answering machine said the boys would be home at 3:00. She glanced at the clock. Just 2:00. "Fiddle! I could get an extra hour in at the Academy if I didn't have to wait for them."

The message had also said she was to make tacos for dinner. DJ got the hamburger browning and headed upstairs to change into her barn clothes. This way she at least had a head start on the cooking.

While she waited for the boys, she checked the air on their bike tires. Since she was the only one around to feed the horses, they would have to ride to Briones with her. They'd ridden to Gran's before with Robert, so she knew they could pedal that far. Thank goodness it wasn't raining.

But . . . she hadn't asked permission to take them there. And what would they do while she worked Patches and fed all three horses? Not that it would take a whole lot of time. But she usually worked Patches for an hour.

So what was wrong with the plan? Nothing, except she hadn't asked in advance.

But how was she supposed to ask in advance when she hadn't known about the problem? Should she try calling Robert? Pull him out of a meeting? Or her mother?

That would be the day.

"Come on, guys. We're going to the Academy." Her announcement brought them up short. She waved good-bye to the woman who dropped them off and turned back to see two startled faces.

"How we getting there?"

"Bikes."

"Yeah!" The two dropped their papers from kindergarten and ran in a circle around the kitchen. "We're going to the barn with DJ."

"Cool it! And get your boots on. It'll be muddy up there." Within minutes the three were pedaling up the street. Halfway up the hill, the boys had to dismount and push their bikes. DJ shifted into low gear and rode beside them.

"Hey, guys, you'd have more breath for pedaling if you'd quit talking so much." She was sorry as soon as the words passed her lips. She held up a hand. "Sorry. I'm just in a hurry 'cause I have lots to do."

"We go downhill now."

"That's faster."

They hopped back on and took off ahead of her, as if to show her how fast they really could pedal. At the Academy they left their bikes beside the barn and walked through the open doors.

"Hey, how come you brought the munchkins?" Tony Andrada, one of the other students, strolled out of the tack room, his saddle on his arm.

"Baby-sitting."

"We's not babies." Four fists clamped on two sets of hips. They sent DJ and Tony equal glares.

"Sorry." DJ realized she was saying that a lot today.

"Have fun." Tony winked at her and ambled off toward his horse's stall.

At least he gets to ride—and train—and— DJ cut off that line of thinking. One thing for sure, she was getting good training in thought control. Now if she could learn to control her mouth, as well.

She knelt in front of the boys. "Okay now. I have work to do, and the best way you can help me is to stay out of the way."

"Good idea. Put 'em to work," Tony called over his shoulder.

"Grandpa Joe lets us clean out Major's and Ranger's stalls."

"Okay, I'll put the horses out on the hot walker and you can clean out their stalls. I'm sure GJ did that already this morning, but you can clean out the dirty shavings."

"And the 'nure."

DJ got them set up with the wheelbarrow and shovels. She didn't dare give them pitchforks. All she needed right now was a stabbed and bleeding brother. "Now, when you've got that loaded, what are you going to do?"

"Ask someone to dump it for us."

"Right. And then what?"

"Put clean shavings in the wheelbarrow."

"And?"

"Ask someone to bring it back."

"Good. Now, you work here and don't go anywhere else. Stay out of everyone's way. Got that?"

They both nodded up at her, then shot each other matching grins. "We get to clean Major's stall."

"That's right, DJ. Start 'em young," another student worker said with a wave.

"DJ?" one of the twins asked.

The other finished, "Can we ride Major when we's done?"

DJ nodded. "Sounds fair to me."

She forced herself to take her time with Patches and keep him calm. Doing so took all her concentration. When he acted up with his usual side steps and crow hops, she forgot about the boys until she rode back to the barn. She put Patches away with an extra horse cookie for good behavior and walked out the rear door and up to Major's stall.

The dirty bedding was gone, and so were the boys.

4

PANIC STRUCK LIKE A RAP ON THE HEAD with a two-by-four.

DJ headed down the aisle toward the dump pile. Where were the twins?

She had just turned the corner when she saw them. The wheelbarrow lay on its side in the middle of the aisle, with the two of them trying to clean up the mess and fill it again. She sucked in a deep breath. They were safe; that was all that mattered, right? Then why did she feel like yanking them up by their jackets and shaking them till their teeth rattled?

"What happened, guys?" Keeping her voice calm took about as much strength as keeping Patches from a dead run.

"It dumped over."

"Why didn't you ask for help like I told you?"

The two boys shook their heads in perfect sync. "No one to ask."

"Come on, Carlos was in the other aisle."

"You said not to leave the stall, but then we couldn't get help and you said you was in a hurry and—"

DJ held up a hand to stop the flood of words. Yelling at them wouldn't do any good or be fair. "Let's get this dumped so you can load fresh shavings while I feed the horses."

"You gonna help us?"

"Yup, I'll wheel the barrow."

When the mess was cleaned up and dumped, she left them loading the wheelbarrow with fresh shavings. "Now stay here. You got that?"

"Yes, but we—"

"No, fill this and then stay." She felt as though she were giving a dog instructions. Sit. Stay. Down, boy.

She filled the water buckets with fresh water, measured the grain, and refilled both horses' hay slings. When she returned to the shavings mound, the twins had filled the wheelbarrow and were now rolling in the fresh shavings, scattering them out to get wet and trampled when it rained again.

Another sigh. "Okay, now sweep those shavings back up in the pile. We don't want to waste any." They did as told, glancing at her out of the corners of their eyes. Flushed red cheeks told of their fun. A shavings curl clung to one blue stocking cap. Bits of shavings decorated their jackets, pants, and boots. She needed a broom to sweep them off.

"How would you like a ride back?" She almost looked around to see who had said that. Here she was trying to be firm with them, and her mouth played tricks on her.

At the delight on their faces, let alone their squeals, she was glad her mouth sometimes did things on its own. Only problem was that too often it got her in trouble.

She lifted the boys to the top of the wheelbarrow and with a grunt got the thing going and trundled back to the stalls. She dumped the boys out with the shavings, making them laugh and shout again.

"You spread that around and I'll go get Major and Ranger. Put some in Ranger's stall, too." Both horses nickered for her when she approached the hot walker. Was there any better sound than a horse nickering a greeting?

Halfway home, thoughts of Robert made her slow, then stop pedaling. What if he got all bent out of shape because she took the boys to the Academy? But he hadn't said she couldn't. But then, she hadn't asked. Now what should she do?

"Why we stopping?" one of the Bs asked, looking up at her.

"Uh, you know what? How about not telling your dad about going to the Academy on the bikes until I have a chance to talk to him."

The boys looked at each other and shrugged.

"Okay?"

" 'Kay."

Later, just as she was serving the tacos, DJ heard tires screeching and the Bronco roaring into the drive.

"Daddy's home!" The boys bailed off their chairs and raced to the front door.

"Bobby, Billy, thank God you are all right." Robert came into the dining room with a boy under each arm. "DJ, where were you?"

She looked up from putting cheese into a taco shell. "Here, why?" *Uh-oh, trouble in town*. His face looked like a thunderstorm had taken up residence.

"I called and called here, and no one answered. I thought something had happened to all of you."

The boys squirmed until he set them down. They looked up at him, then to DJ. "We's fine, Daddy."

"I see that. Darla Jean?"

"We rode over to the Academy to take care of the horses. I asked Amy to do it, but she had to go to her grandma's and there wasn't anyone else."

"Why didn't you call me?"

"You said you had an important meeting. I didn't want to bother you." DJ wanted to stamp her feet and yell right back at him. "If I'd known in advance, I could have made other arrangements, but . . ."

Robert swept his hair back with the palm of his hand. "DJ, don't you understand that you and the boys are more important to me than any meeting?" He took in a deep breath and lowered his voice. "Thank God the traffic was light on the San Mateo bridge, or I'd have run right up and over the cars. I almost called the police to come by here and check on the house to see if it was still standing." He swiped his hand over his hair again. "I even called your mother to see if she knew anything."

DJ felt like a huge fist socked her in the gut. *Now I'm in for it.* "I . . . I'm sorry. I did what I thought best."

"We helped DJ at the barn."

"We cleaned Major's stall. . . ."

"And Ranger's, and we . . ."

"Spilled the 'nure and . . ."

"Played in the shavings . . ."

"And rode the bikes . . ."

"And how come . . .

"You yelled at DJ?" The two advanced on their father like miniature bulldogs.

"Whoa." Robert took a step backward. He held up his hands, palms out to ward them off.

"DJ gave us a ride in the barrel. . . ."

"And Major snuffed my hair—"

"Barrel?" Robert looked at the boys, then DJ.

"Wheelbarrow?" DJ asked.

They nodded . . . hard.

"Can we have a barrel, Daddy?"

Robert nodded, his lips reluctantly curving in a grin. "I think we have three or four of them on my jobs. We'll have one at the new house."

"And the barn and a pony and Major and—" The boys danced around the room.

"Hey, guys, your dinner is ready. Come and eat." DJ set their plates at their places. "You want tacos?" She looked up at Robert.

"Sure. I was supposed to have dinner with the client but . . ."

DJ flinched. "Sorry."

After he'd taken his place and was dishing up his meal, he looked up at her. "You know, if something like this happens again and you can't get hold of me, leave a message on the answering machine here and I'll check for that. Also, you can leave a message on my cell phone, and when I turn it on again, I'll get it."

"Okay. I guess I'm just not used to all that fancy phone stuff."

As they finished eating, DJ said, "The boys need to get used to being at the barns, though, if they're going to show their horses someday."

"Horses?" One eyebrow cocked.

"Sure, two boys, two horses. Otherwise we can't all ride up in Briones together."

"Two horses. Two horses." Two voices chanted as one.

The phone rang and Robert answered it. The tone of his voice immediately told DJ it was her mother on the other end. She nodded over her shoulder, and she and the boys picked up their plates and tiptoed out of the room.

"You guys go watch TV or a video so I can get my homework done." She motioned them toward their room. "Your dad'll come for you later."

"But, DJ—"

"No buts." *There they go with their whipped-puppy looks again.* DJ kept a stern look on her face. "Come on, guys. If I don't get my homework done, I'll never get to ride Major again."

"We could ride him for you."

"Thanks anyway."

"When we gonna dye Easter eggs?"

"Tomorrow."

They looked at her again over their shoulders, as if hoping she had relented.

She shook her head. Would they never give up? When they finally went in their room, she did the same. The stack of books on her desk hadn't moved. She threw herself across her bed and let her eyelids drift closed.

She woke sometime later to Robert shaking her shoulder.

"You better get in bed, DJ. It's nearly midnight."

She groaned and rolled over. "I only wanted to rest my eyes a few minutes. Now I've wasted the whole evening."

"You must have needed the sleep. Your mom will be home about noon. I think I'll take the boys to meet her at the airport. You can come with us or get your stuff done at the Academy so we can dye eggs later in the afternoon."

DJ shook her head, trying to wake up enough to be able to answer. "Thought I'd get all my homework done tonight so I wouldn't have to think about it this weekend. Guess I better get right home from chores and do that."

"Okay. I have one favor, though. I forgot to buy eggs tonight, so could you wait until I get back from the grocery store before you leave in the morning?"

"Sure."

"I'll go real early." He scrubbed a hand across his eyes. "I'd go now, but I'm beat." He laid a hand on her shoulder. "Night, daughter. Sorry I yelled at you."

"That's okay." DJ yawned so big she feared her jaw would break. After Robert left the room, she shucked her clothes and, with her eyes refusing to stay open, pulled on her nightshirt and crawled under the covers. She was asleep before she could even turn out her lamp.

She woke to the phone ringing. When no one answered, she leaped out of bed and dashed into her mother's empty room. At the same time as she wondered, *Where's Robert?* she remembered he was going for eggs. Or at least she thought she remembered him talking about that.

"Hello."

"DJ, this is Bridget. Do not panic. There is nothing wrong."

Bridget had read her mind. The sound of her trainer's voice had sent instant panic surging through DJ, snapping her entirely awake like a bucket of cold water in the face.

"Okay."

"I was wondering if you could be here at nine. Mrs. Johnson will be here, and we could talk with her about selling Patches. I looked at a horse yesterday over in Marin County that might be perfect for her."

DJ glanced at the clock. 7:30. "Sure I'll be there, but . . ." She paused a moment to collect her thoughts. "But why me?"

Bridget chuckled, a warm sound that made DJ smile inside. "You, ma petite, are the trainer, no?"

"Yes, but . . ." She wanted to say "I'm just a kid" but refrained.

"No buts. This way she can ask you questions about Patches. No one knows that horse like you do."

"I'm going to miss him." DJ realized how true that was as she said the words. Patches was a challenge every day, and she'd learned a lot training him. And his owner.

"See you at nine." Bridget hung up before DJ could respond.

"DJ, where's Daddy?" a sleepy voice from the doorway asked.

"And Mommy?"

"Your dad's at the grocery store, and Mom's not back yet. You guys better get your slippers on. It's cold in here."

"You don't have slippers on."

DJ groaned. "Yeah, and my feet are freezing." She clapped her hands and grabbed at them. "I'm gonna get you if you don't watch out."

They ran shrieking down the hall, giving her time to slip into the bathroom and slam the door shut.

"And so it is my opinion that you should sell Patches and purchase a horse you could enjoy more."

And be safer with. But DJ only nodded when Mrs. Johnson looked at her.

"Surely this isn't necessary." Mrs. Johnson shook her head, looking from Bridget to DJ and back again. "You don't just sell a horse because he's spirited, do you? Why, Patches is my friend. He nickers when he sees me coming and . . ." She leaned back in her chair and crossed her arms, then shifted again when the cast on her arm caused her discomfort.

Bridget looked from the casted arm up to Mrs. Johnson's eyes without saying a word.

"But I'm becoming a better rider, and DJ . . ." She sent DJ a pleading look.

"I . . . I wish we could say something different, but Patches always gives me a hard time, too. When you count them, he's dumped me more times than you."

"And that is only because you have ridden him so little, Mrs. Johnson. Think how much more pleasure you had when you rode the schooling horses." Bridget leaned forward, elbows on her desk, hands folded.

"But Patches is mine, the first horse I've ever owned."

DJ could hear the sorrow in the woman's voice. And the stubbornness. "What about Andrew?" she asked.

"Andrew isn't riding Patches."

"No. But he is so frightened for you that he's back to being afraid of Bandit again, too. He's worked hard to get over that fear just because he knows how happy it will make you. He was even beginning to look forward to riding up in Briones with all the family."

Mrs. Johnson groaned and looked at the floor. The silence in the office made the normal noises of whinnying horses and riders calling to each other seem loud. When she looked up again, sadness dimmed her eyes. "Let me talk to my husband first, okay?"

Bridget nodded. "Of course. But I want you to know that I have found a horse I think would suit you well. You would be wise to go with me to at least look at it."

"Thank you, I guess." The woman tried to put a smile on her face. "Guess I'll go give Patches a treat and be on my way, then." She got to her feet, not standing nearly as erect as when she came in. "See you later."

DJ watched her walk out of the room, wishing she could run over and say, "Hey, forget it. We'll make Patches behave so you can keep him."

"This is the best thing to do." Bridget's voice carried all the assurance of her years of working with both horses and humans.

"I guess." DJ sighed and heaved herself to her feet. "I better go finish up and get home."

"Any idea when you will be riding again?"

"Soon, I hope. This is driving me crazy, and if Mrs. Johnson decides to sell Patches, I won't have anything to ride."

"You want Omega back?"

DJ thought a moment. Without Patches to train, she would have more time for Major and more time for her homework, too. They had said they'd take care of the rest of her expenses. "I'll talk with Mom and Robert, but I bet they'll say no."

"That is good." Bridget pulled out the pencil she always kept tucked in the side of her hair. "It takes a great deal of support, both personal and financial, for a rider to make it into the big time. I am glad to see you are getting that."

"Thanks. See ya." DJ left the office. She could always go back to mucking stalls if she needed to. But teaching and training were much more fun. Maybe once in a while she could take that extra hour and go ride up in Briones. She glanced up at the hills to see fog blanketing the top halves and wisping around the lower trees. Riding into fog like that would be spooky—and fun. She sighed. Two stalls to clean and she was outta there.

The others weren't home yet when she got there, so she made her bed and picked up her room before settling down to the stack of homework. She needed to decide on a topic for her history term paper, and another book report was due in English, besides her journal. She hadn't written in that for three days again. Plus she had two short essays to write. What a fun Saturday this would be.

She put the algebra book at the bottom of the stack. Robert *had* agreed to help her with that. And he wasn't here now.

So get it done and show him you can do it yourself. There was that bossy little voice again. She tried to ignore it, then slammed her English book closed and jerked out the math. If that little voice was indeed the Holy Spirit prompting her like Gran said, maybe she'd better learn to listen.

"Heavenly Father, you know how much I ha—ah, dislike algebra. Please help me get this stuff into my head and then keep it there. My verse says 'I can do all things through Christ who strengthens me,' and I am trying to believe that. Even algebra, huh?" She waited. How come that little voice came at other times but not when she wanted an answer?

"Thanks, I guess." She scrunched her mouth back and forth. "Amen."

She could hear Robert's voice in her ear. *"Now, read very carefully right from the beginning and then read it again. You can understand this. I know you can."*

By the time she heard the twins come yelling "DJ!" through the front door, she'd finished her algebra—with questions for Robert on two of the problems and one principle—caught up on her journal, and roughed out one essay.

She rose and stretched, locking her hands high above her head and twisting so she could pull all the kinks out. "I'm up here."

The two rocketed through the door. "Come on, we get to dye Easter eggs."

"Mommy said you make bee-ew-tiful eggs. Come on."

They grabbed her hands and pulled her out the door.

DJ pretended to dig in her heels. "Help, I'm being kidnapped by munchkins!"

The rainbow-hued eggs filled two large baskets by the time they quit. The plastic-covered table looked like they'd had a dye fight. Stickers lay in puddles of dye, and wax crayons were worn to the nub. Robert held a blue egg up to the light.

"You think it could use a sticker or two?"

"Good luck." Lindy brought a sponge from the kitchen.

Billy or Bobby peeled a basket sticker off his sweat shirt. "Here's one."

DJ pointed to the cups of dye. "You guys dump those in the sink and I'll—"

"No. I think they've dumped enough." Robert looked over the tops of his glasses to the twins. They giggled.

"Only tipped one cup over."

"And that was an accident."

"Oh sure. I think you did it on purpose."

"Daddy." Hands on hips.

"Okay, I'll dump the dye and you guys pick up the stuff." DJ swept the littered table with an open hand.

"Save the stickers," said Bobby—at least, DJ thought it must be Bobby since he usually spoke first and liked to save things.

Lindy groaned. "I don't think so. I'll bring the trash bag and you can dump things right in it."

When the dining room looked normal again, even with the silk tulips in a vase in the center of the table, they all gathered in the family room, the adults with coffee and the kids with sodas.

"I have news for all of you," Lindy said, leaning back against the sofa and smiling at Robert.

"What?" He smiled back.

They're going to get mushy again. DJ rolled her eyes so far up that she caught a glimpse of her eyebrows.

"I announced last night at the meeting that I am taking a leave of absence so I'll be home to take care of the boys." She smiled at the twins. "Starting Monday."

"You can *do* that?" DJ blurted out.

"I did." Lindy reached for the boys and pulled them onto her lap. "And it feels wonderful." She hugged the boys and kissed their cheeks.

DJ couldn't believe her ears. *Her* mother taking time off.

She *never* missed work—even when she'd had pneumonia one time.

She never took time off work for me. DJ could feel her smile wobble. If this was what jealousy felt like, no wonder God said it wasn't a good idea.

5

"DJ, DARLIN', YOU DON'T LOOK VERY HAPPY."

"Oh." DJ tried to paste a smile on her face, but the glue refused to stick.

"So what's wrong?" Gran and Joe looked at her, both of them waiting for an answer.

If only it were that easy to explain how she felt. She wished she could run and hide her face against Gran's painting smock like she used to. Being taller than her grandmother made that seem a bit foolish now.

Since the Easter sunrise service was one of DJ's favorites, she had gone with her grandparents, and they were now sitting in the kitchen at Gran's. Any minute Lindy would call and say to come for the Easter egg hunt. GJ had gone over and hid the eggs earlier while the boys were still asleep. After the hunt they'd all go back to church for the regular service.

DJ wanted nothing more than to head for the hills, on Major's back, of course.

She drew designs on the tablecloth with her fingernail. *How do you tell your grandmother that you're a spoiled brat who's jealous of two small boys? Now, if that doesn't sound great.*

"Mom's taking a leave of absence from work."

49

"Wonderful. I didn't think that day would ever happen." Gran leaned forward and reached across the table to still DJ's busy hand. "So why aren't you happy with that? Now you won't have to worry about taking care of the boys when Robert is too busy." DJ had told them of the boys' time at the barns.

DJ shrugged. "I don't know."

"Sure you do. Let's just figure it out." Joe went into his interrogator mode.

DJ sent him a halfhearted glare. He winked at her, which made a three-quarter-strength glare easier.

The phone rang and she breathed a sigh of relief.

"They're ready to hunt eggs. Let's go." Joe hung up the phone and took Gran's and DJ's coats off the wall pegs. "Tell me quick so you can have a fun day." He kept his attention on DJ even as he helped Gran into her coat.

DJ wanted to crawl under the table. How come she could never get away with a bad mood like other kids did?

"Well?" Joe ushered them out and shut the door.

"Isn't the sun grand? It really feels like spring." Gran lifted her face to the warmth and winked at DJ.

"Uh-huh. Come clean, kid."

Distracting Joe was like trying to pull a bloodhound off a scent.

DJ jerked the car door open. "She takes time off for the boys but can't even remember to ask me if I—if I—"

"Ah, nobody loves me, everybody hates me, think I'll go boil up some worms, pour fudge sauce on them, and . . ." Joe continued nodding as he slid behind the wheel.

DJ wavered between the burning behind her eyes and a giggle at Joe's messed-up verse. She sniffed and dug in her pocket for a tissue.

"You're right, darlin'. Your mother never did take time off if you got sick or something. But that was because I was there and we needed the money. Now she can because Robert—"

"It wasn't just the money. She didn't want to. Her job and school were always more important than me." The words came out in a rush, along with tears that must have been hiding for a long time, considering the way they gushed down her face.

"Ah, I was afraid you felt that way." Gran turned in her seat and reached for DJ's hand. "But I hoped that if I loved you enough you'd get by."

"Gran, you did. It's not your fault I'm being a brat. I keep telling myself that this is stupid and I . . ." DJ leaned her cheek against the back of her grandmother's hand. Gran's rosewater hand lotion smelled of love and forever.

"Ah, darlin', knowing what you feel is important so we can talk about it and let the bad feelings go away. So you feel hurt . . ."

"And jealous . . ."

"And left out . . ."

The two of them almost sounded like the twins in finishing each other's sentences. DJ sniffed again.

"And tired of being a brat."

"Ah, DJ, you have always been honest, almost painfully so. Don't be too hard on yourself. This is all part and parcel of growing up. Do you know that your mother loves you?"

DJ nodded. "I . . . I guess so."

"Do you think you could tell her how you feel?"

DJ shook her head. "She'd go ballistic and then Robert would get all bent out of shape and the twins and I'd cry and it would be a big mess."

"Okay for now. But I think this is something that has to be worked on." Joe glanced at her in the rearview mirror. "But you better know for absolutely certain sure that I love you, your grandmother adores you, and God says you are one of His most treasured kids. Got that?"

DJ sent him a slightly watery smile. "Yes, sir!" Sniffing and blowing her nose somehow spoiled the effect.

"Good. You okay?"

She thought a moment, then nodded. "I guess." The cloud that had been hanging over her head had melted away. The sun was shining, not only outside but in the car, too. Shining so brightly she had to blink.

Joe had hardly set the brake before the twins shrieked to a stop beside the car.

"Grandma, Grandpa, DJ, hurry."

"The Easter Bunny came."

"With baskets . . ."

"And a chocolate bunny . . ."

"And we gotta hunt for the eggs."

They grabbed Joe's hand as soon as he opened the car door.

"Easy now." Joe scooped them up, one under each arm like their father did, only Joe grunted at the effort. "Either you guys are getting too big for this, or I'm getting too old."

They giggled and squirmed, leading the way for DJ and Gran to follow.

Robert met them at the door. "Dad—"

"Don't say it." Joe set the boys down and sucked in a deep breath. "I must be getting out of shape."

The boys grabbed her hand and yelled, "Come on, DJ. You gots to help us find the eggs."

"Thank goodness you came quickly," Robert said under his breath. "I don't think I could have lasted another minute."

Lindy strolled down the stairs, dressed for church in a cream suit with a mint green shell. Every hair lay in place as if it didn't dare move. She finished clipping the back on her earring and smiled at Joe and Gran. "Happy Easter." She gave them each a kiss on the cheek and turned to DJ. "Couldn't you wear a dress on Easter, at least?"

DJ clenched her teeth and her fists, backing up just enough that the kiss missed her cheek. "Happy Easter to you, too, Mother." Shooting her grandmother a glance that screamed, *See?* she followed the boys outside.

"Come on, DJ, we got three hundred eggs to find."

"No, we don't. We only dyed thirty. Remember, you broke some?"

"Oh, but it's lots." They made sure she had a basket, too, and headed for the flower beds and shrubs.

Shouting at each found treasure, they ran and darted across the yard, looking under and in bushes, up into the trees and through the grass. DJ followed behind.

"Hey, you missed one." She stopped under the Liquid-ambar tree and looked at the joint of branch and trunk.

"You get it," Bobby or Billy squealed when they found a nest with two eggs in it.

"There just happens to be a couple of plastic eggs with something inside *you'd* appreciate," Robert said from right behind her.

DJ took the bright pink plastic egg out of the crook in the tree and shook it. A scraping sound came with the action. She hung the basket on her arm and twisted the egg open. A twenty-dollar bill fell, but she caught it before it touched the ground.

"Thank you." She grinned up at him.

"Beats chocolate, huh?"

She tipped her head and squinted her eyes as if she had a hard time making the decision. "I guess, but not by much."

"Good, 'cause there's a two-foot bunny back in the house with your name on it. Don't eat it all at once."

"I won't. Are there more of these?" She held up her egg.

"I ain't tellin'." Robert winked at her as he left in answer to a plea from one of the boys.

By the time they'd found all the eggs and devoured the

cinnamon rolls Gran brought, it was time to leave for church again.

Seated in the pew between Robert and Gran, DJ tried to ignore the feeling that was doing its best to tie her stomach up in square knots and slipknots and even a hangman's knot. She should have put on a dress; she knew that when she got out of bed.

But when she looked, her one dress was wrinkled from being smashed into the *other* end of her closet. The end where she stored the clothes she didn't like or that didn't fit anymore.

Besides that, she'd been running late. She'd put on her dress slacks and a sky-blue shirt with a navy sweater and thought it looked pretty good. Gran had said so, too.

But her mother didn't think so. DJ stared at the white lilies lining the altar rail. Why were clothes so important, after all? No, she didn't look like her mother. Her mother would look good in one of the feed sacks they had over at the barn, and they were made out of paper. But DJ's clothes were clean, with no holes, and besides, her mother had bought the blue blouse and sweater for her.

Good thing I'm going to Brad's on Tuesday. Now, if I can just keep out of a fight so I don't get grounded worse. Spring Break started on Monday, and if her mother was going to be home . . .

She stood with the others to sing the final hymn. *Sorry, God, for letting my mind wander, but I did pay attention in the first service. Thanks for sending Jesus. And if you could keep me from mouthing off at my mother for the next couple of days, I'd sure appreciate it. How come she doesn't like me much?*

After church she met Amy at the bottom of the front steps. "Hey, you look cool."

Amy smoothed the front of her green lace-trimmed dress. "You like it?"

"Sure is different. And a hat even. It keeps the sun from reflecting off your braces and blinding everyone."

Amy rolled her eyes and shook her head. "So are we going to the printer tomorrow to get our note cards re-done?"

"Guess so. You got your half of the money?"

Amy nodded. She waved at her mother calling her from the sidewalk. "I gotta go. Right after chores, okay?"

By evening, DJ and the twins were experiencing sugar overload. Half a giant chocolate bunny plus various other goodies would do that to you.

Monday morning she felt marginally better. By the time they ordered enough note cards for four dozen packets and Amy had ordered reprints of her pictures to glue on hers, they counted only two dollars left between them.

"I guess we could split a Jamoca almond fudge malt at the B and R," DJ said, counting her change once again. "Sure hope these all sell fast. My bank account is now screaming with hunger pangs."

"Malt sounds good. Maybe that'll stop the screaming." Amy patted her flat middle. "Of my stomach, anyway, not my account." She unlocked her bike and, keeping one foot on the curb, swung the other over the seat. "If you're going to be gone, we can't put the packages together until next week."

"I know. But I'm staying at Brad's as long as I can. At this rate Stormy is going to be half grown before I get to see her again." Stormy was the registered Arabian filly her father had given her after the big flood at his farm earlier in the year. She'd been right there with the mare when Stormy was born and helped keep the baby alive when she wouldn't, or rather couldn't, nurse.

"Get me some pictures of her, will you?" Amy pushed off. "Race you."

At the Academy later, Bridget motioned DJ to come to the office. "Mrs. Johnson is selling Patches, so you will not need to train him any longer."

"That's good, I guess." DJ slid down in the chair.

"She is going with me to look at the other horse, too." Bridget picked up an envelope from under some papers on her desk. "She said to give you this."

DJ reached for the envelope. "What is it?"

"I do not know. Open it." Bridget pushed her half glasses up on her nose.

DJ slit the envelope and drew out a folded piece of paper. She scanned the typed page and held the check between two fingers. "She wants a drawing of Patches, eighteen by twenty-four or bigger and done right away. She's paying me—" DJ choked on the amount—"two hundred dollars. Bridget, that's too much."

"Oh, I have a feeling part of that money is her way of thanking your for your work with her and Patches, too."

"But . . . but she already paid me for that." DJ looked from the letter to Bridget and back to the check. "You think I should try to give it back? Maybe she just made a mistake."

Bridget shook her head, smiling at the same time. "You have earned every dime of it. Now go. I have work to do."

After telling Amy what happened, DJ jumped on her bike and headed home for her drawing pad and pencils. She'd use the time she'd slotted for training Patches to draw him instead.

That evening after the dinner table was cleared and devotions finished, Robert leaned back in his chair. "I've got good news for us."

The boys stopped poking each other and giggling. "What news?"

"We are moving into the new house on Thursday."

"Yay! New house, new house." The boys high-fived each other and jumped down to run around the table and hug their father.

"Isn't that wonderful?" Lindy leaned over and pecked Robert on the cheek. The boys immediately wormed their way into her arms, and she smiled down at them. "You get your new playroom. How about that?"

"DJ?" Robert looked over at her, one eyebrow quirked in question.

"I . . . I won't be here. Brad's picking me up tomorrow."

"Oh, that's right." Robert smacked his forehead with the heel of his hand. "I forgot. Sorry. Well, no problem. The movers are going to take care of everything anyway. They'll be here on Wednesday to pack and move things over on Thursday. If there's anything you don't want packed, make sure you get rid of it before you leave."

"What about my posters and pictures and stuff?"

"They'll do a better job than any of us. They're trained to do it all."

"I can't believe it. I don't have to pack the kitchen." Lindy tickled one of the boys on the nose.

DJ looked at her. She'd lived in this house all her life, and Gran said they'd moved into this house when Lindy was a teenager. She'd never moved anything. So why the big deal?

Why was DJ being so critical? She kept her mouth shut by clamping her teeth together. No smart remarks.

"Do you have a problem with that?" Robert asked softly, letting Lindy play with the boys.

"N-no, I guess not. Just took me by surprise."

"But we've been counting the days."

"I know." DJ shrugged. "But it's different thinking about it, and then all of a sudden the movers are coming and I'm going to be gone."

"I wish I were going to be gone." Robert rolled his eyes. "Moving is a pain no matter how many movers there are. You can come home to it all finished. Lucky girl."

DJ spent the evening sorting things out of her closet. She put all the clothes that were too small for her in a garbage bag to donate to charity, along with some stuffed animals she no longer wanted. She sorted through a box of old school papers and tossed all but the drawings and special projects. Down on the bottom of her bookshelf, she found a scrapbook Gran had given her and taped all her artwork on to the heavy pages. By the time she was done, the scrapbook lay wider than her hand's width. Gran had done the same with her things from early grade school.

She pulled that book off the shelf and flipped through the pages. Some of the drawings made her grin. But Gran said to keep them. They all showed her promise as an artist. One of stick figures beside a house made her shake her head. If *that* was the beginning of great art, she'd eat the book.

With her sorting finished, she went back to the picture she'd started of Patches. She'd drawn him while he played on the hot walker, half rearing with one front foot slashing the air and his mane flying as he tossed his head.

She cleaned up some lines and worked on the shading, trying to get his muscles just right, all the while humming under her breath.

"You sound happy," her mother said from the doorway. "What are you working on?"

DJ propped the bottom of the pad on her knee and stared at it with her eyes half closed. "A picture of Patches.

Mrs. Johnson asked me to do one."

"May I see?"

"Sure, come on in."

"Oh, DJ, that's beautiful." Lindy stood behind her daughter so she could look over her shoulder. "Wait until Gran sees this."

"It's not done yet." DJ brushed some bits of eraser off the page. She cocked her head. "Something about his ears and that off back foot isn't right yet."

"Maybe so, but you sure got the devil dancing in his eyes."

"He's not mean—intentionally, that is." DJ studied the drawing some more. "I'm sure going to miss him."

"Miss him?"

"Mrs. Johnson is selling him. Bridget and I talked her into it so she can buy a horse she can enjoy. Bridget found her another horse if she likes it."

"When did all this come about?" Lindy sat down on the end of the bed.

"Last couple of days." DJ erased one ear and started again. This time the angle worked right. "Ah good."

"Robert says you're catching on to the algebra."

"Umm." She drew the line of the leg, erased it, and drew it again.

"We talked it over and decided that you are indeed trying your best and that your grade will change soon, so you can consider yourself off restrictions."

"Umm." DJ nodded and mumbled at the same time. She redrew the hoof and a couple of lines under it to show motion. "There."

She blinked and turned to her mother, who leaned back on the bed, hands clasped around one raised knee. "What did you say?"

Lindy repeated herself.

DJ let out a whoop and leaped to her feet, her pencils

and eraser flying every which way. "Thank you, oh thank you, thank you, thank you!"

"I take it you told her," Robert said from the doorway.

"Whatever gave you that idea?"

DJ had a hard time settling back down to work on the drawing after Robert and Lindy left the room. Finally, *finally* she could ride Major again.

She stopped. And now she was going to be gone. She raised her hands and let them fall. "Fiddle. Fiddle, fiddle, fiddle."

6

"JOE! JOE, HE'S LIMPING."

Joe came out of Ranger's stall just as DJ walked Major into his. "So the old injury is kicking up, eh?" Joe ran his hand down Major's front leg, feeling for any heat or swelling. "I don't feel anything. When did it start?"

"I warmed him up real slow like I always do, then we did a lot of flatwork, reviewing the drills we'd been working on. And then I couldn't stand it anymore. I had to try just one jump." She stroked Major's nose and rubbed his ears while she talked. "He was doing great. Then something happened. I could feel it, like he almost stumbled but not quite—really weird. He ticked the jump and started limping."

Joe squatted beside Major and examined both front legs again. "Nothing. It must be in his shoulder. Trot him down the aisle and back."

DJ trotted him away, stopped, and returned. "See, I told you. First time I have him out. What could have happened? He wasn't that bad out of shape, was he?"

Joe shook his head. "I've been riding him, you know. Not like you do but enough to keep him limber, and you've been lunging him. That's not the problem." Joe stroked down Major's shoulder. "Let's get the liniment and start an ice pack. He'll be right as rain in a day or two."

"But I'm leaving this afternoon." She put her arms around Major's neck and leaned against him. The big horse whuffled down her back and nosed her ponytail. When he blew on her neck, she giggled. "That tickles, you big silly."

She pulled back and looked at Joe. "Maybe I better stay home. I can call Brad and tell him I can't come."

"All because of a little limp?" Joe shook his head. "I don't think so. I'll take care of him. It isn't the first time and surely won't be the last."

"But that's not fair—to you, I mean. He's my horse and my responsibility."

"You have an even more important responsibility—to your dad. Now, let's get this old son taken care of."

After they'd rubbed in the liniment, DJ watched Major pull hay out of the sling and chew. "He doesn't seem to be in pain."

"It would have to be mighty bad before he'd let on. This guy's got a heart as big as California. Even when he was shot in the shoulder, he kept on going until he collapsed. Saved my life, he did."

DJ loved hearing stories from Joe's days in the mounted police. She traced the scar where the bullet had hit Major instead of Joe. "You suppose that old injury could be causing problems now? It is the same shoulder."

"Nope. Now, if the bullet had hit bone, it might be different, but it was all soft tissue. I don't know; he could be developing some arthritis or some such, but I think he just stepped wrong and got a bit of a sprain. You watch—he'll be fine by the time you get home."

Later, when he came to pick up DJ, Brad stopped by the Academy and checked the shoulder, saying the same things as Joe. "Rest and then gentle exercise are what he needs."

DJ felt like screaming. *But he's been resting. And now I can finally ride again. We have shows coming up, and I thought I had him in top condition. Why would stepping wrong cause this?*

In the Land Rover on the way to Santa Rosa, Brad reached over and patted DJ's hand. "You're worried about Major, aren't you?"

"Trying not to. I just can't understand why this happened."

"DJ, horses are like people. They get injured and they get well. Sometimes you can get whiplash stepping wrong off a step. Being in good condition helps, but accidents still happen."

"You really don't think this is going to be an ongoing problem?"

"Well, I can't say for sure. Sometimes an injury, an old one—"

"Like that mud slide in Briones. I knew it. . . ."

"As I was saying, sometimes an injury leaves a weakness that flares up again. Like a person who repeatedly sprains the same ankle. The ankle is weak—they say it takes two years for a sprained ankle to really heal and be as strong as it was before."

"Yuck. Remind me not to sprain my ankle."

"Listen, if this does become a recurring problem, you always have Herndon to fall back on."

"But he's a dressage horse—"

"Who loves to jump." Brad checked over his shoulder to change lanes. "He would have made a much better jumper than a dressage horse. That's why Jackie changed mounts. He just didn't have what it takes to go Grand Prix, and that's what she wants to do."

DJ watched his face in the light from the dashboard. Man, her father was one handsome dude. She rolled her lips together to keep the grin from showing. Funny, it seemed like she'd known him much longer than the few months since he'd called to say he was her biological father and wanted to meet her. Her love of horses came from him for sure.

"So what's gone on since I was up here last?"

"It seems like a year ago. Let's see, we have four new babies, two more mares to foal. Mares are coming in to breed to Matadorian, and this will be our first year to use Sheik, our younger stallion. We went to the show in Phoenix and bought two more mares there. Wait till you see the one called Sea Gypsy. I think she'll match well with Matadorian and throw colts like you wouldn't believe." He turned to look at her. "Sure do wish you wanted to show Arabs."

"I'll learn to show them, but jumping in the Olympics is more important to me."

"Yeah, I know, and there's only so much time."

They talked horses all the way to the turn-in to the farm. Old-fashioned light posts with two globes lined the way from the road up to the house, crowning the top of a rounded hill.

Brad checked his watch. "We've got a few minutes until Jackie has dinner ready. You want to go see your baby first?"

"Need you ask?" DJ sighed. "She's probably forgotten all about me."

"Most likely, but it won't take long to refresh her memory. I've been showing her a picture of you every day so she wouldn't forget."

"Right."

They stopped in front of a long white barn lined with horse stalls on either side of the wide aisle. To the front were the foaling stalls, with only one occupied.

"She should foal while you are here, but that's the man talking, not the mare."

"Dad, is it true that mares in the wild can start and stop the birthing at will if something frightens them?" Calling him Dad surprised her almost as much as it did him.

He smiled at her. "I've heard that, too. Up to a point, I'm sure. But once that foal's feet show, running would kill it." Together they leaned over the half wall of the foaling stall. The mare dozed in the back corner after checking them out with one open eye.

"She sure doesn't seem worried."

"No, Veda, there, is an old hand. This will be her tenth foal."

"Wow. She's getting kind of old."

"Be careful what you say. You don't want to hurt her feelings. Come on, your child awaits."

They could hear horses scrambling to their feet as they approached the stall. The mare came right up to Brad, nosing him for the treats he always carried in his pockets. The filly peeked out from behind her dam, only now she was tall enough that her mother's tail no longer feathered over her face but just draped over her back. She hesitated barely a moment or two before coming forward for her share of the goodies. But she went to Brad, giving DJ a wide berth.

"Hey, Stormy, how you been?" DJ held out a piece of horse cookie.

Stormy ducked under her mother's neck and ignored the offering.

"She is such a cutie. Man, has she grown." DJ patted the mare, hoping her baby would change her mind and come for a reward. "Her mane looks like a shoe brush."

But Stormy ignored her, ducking away as soon as she got her treat from Brad's outstretched hand.

"Jackie's been the one working with her the most, since we thought having her accustomed to a woman might make it easier for you. You watch—by tomorrow she'll be eating out of your hand. If only we could get you up here more often."

"Now with shows starting, my weekends are going to be really busy."

Together the two of them strolled back toward the Land Rover, listening to the horses settle down again. Brad turned off the light and slid the door shut. "Let's go eat."

"Darla Jean Randall, I am so happy to see you I could sing and dance!" Jackie turned from stirring something that smelled wonderful on the stove and gave DJ a big hug. "And if you've heard me sing . . ." She shook her head.

"Not here, I hope." Brad sniffed the garlicky fragrance. "Italian?"

"Your favorite. You want to toss the salad?" She turned the oven dial to Broil. "The bread's already in there." Surveying the kitchen, she put a finger to her chin. "I know I'm forgetting something. Oh, DJ, would you please get the plate of antipasta out of the fridge and set it on the counter. We can munch while we finish up here. So what did you think of her?"

"Stormy?" DJ turned from the refrigerator door. "She's about the cutest thing I've ever seen. She wouldn't come to me, though. Looked at me like, 'Who're you and what do you think you're doing giving my mom treats?' "

"Sounds just like her. She has a mind of her own already. I can't wait to see the two of you in the show-ring."

DJ picked up a carrot stick and an olive. "That means I have to learn to show halter."

"You could use the experience. At the upper-level shows you need to be in every class you can."

DJ groaned. "Halter's boring."

"Says the voice of longtime experience." Brad leaned against the butcher block center island and waved a celery curl as he talked. "You ever shown halter?"

"Once."

"How about riding Hunter Seat?"

"Lots."

"Lots?"

"Three or four times, I guess."

He continued naming classes, and DJ got the idea rather quickly that she had a lot of learning to do. Bridget had said the same thing, but it all seemed in the distant future. According to Brad, that future was roaring closer, like a freight train on the loose.

"I guess we can begin working on some of those things this week." Jackie drained the pasta and flicked off the oven. "You *can* ride again, can't you?"

"Yep." She went on to tell about Major's limp as all three of them put things on the table and sat down.

After Brad said grace and thanked God for bringing DJ back to them, the discussion continued about what DJ needed to learn and how they could help her. The evening passed in a haze of horse talk. When she went to bed, she hugged all the new ideas to herself, thanking her heavenly Father for this man and woman who had come into her life so unexpectedly.

"God, you sure are amazing," DJ whispered in the darkness. "I was so hung up about not wanting a dad in my life, and now I have two. Guess you wanted to make up for lost time, huh?" DJ lay staring into the darkness. "And please take care of Major; make his shoulder all better so we can really begin to work hard." She pressed a hand to her middle. "I get butterflies just thinking about bigger shows."

Brad had plenty of horses for her to practice on. By noon the next day, she felt dizzy from all he'd been cramming into her head. It beat algebra any day. After lunch she sat in the corner of Stormy's stall, waiting for the filly to come to her. The mare settled into a doze after nibbling her share of horse cookies, and while Stormy wanted to ignore DJ, she couldn't.

Closer and closer she'd come, then dart away if DJ made a move. Finally she planted her front feet wide apart and stretched her muzzle as far as she could to reach the treat. One step to go.

"Come on, baby, just an inch or two more."

DJ felt a familiar tickle in her nose. She wrinkled her face, hoping . . .

She sneezed. "Fiddle."

Stormy leaped behind her mother as if she'd been struck by lightning.

"Double fiddle." DJ blew her nose and tucked the tissue back in her pocket. Back to holding out the treat. She needed a brace to prop it up, as long as this was taking. For sure, she needed to come here more often.

Once again, tiptoe, one step at a time.

Her arm wavered.

Reach, r-e-a-c-h. Soft lips tickled the ends of DJ's fingers as the baby took her treat and leaped backward, her hooves slipping and scrambling in the straw.

"Good girl." DJ dug in her pocket and palmed another. "This time you have to come closer to take it."

Stormy munched her goodie and nodded, the star on her nose flashing white with the movement.

"You are so cute. Now, get yourself over here and let's get together." DJ kept up a running patter, all the while forcing herself to wait patiently while she wanted to hug the little soft neck and tickle Stormy's nose. "Sure wish Amy could see you. She'd go nuts with her camera."

When she finally laid a hand on Stormy's neck, DJ felt as though she'd jumped a perfect round of six-foot fences. Not that she'd ever done that, but the thought persisted.

"You are one patient kid," Brad said, leaning on the stall wall. "I was about to come and get her and tie her up so you could play with her. Wait until you see the crop of babies playing in the pasture. What a hoot."

DJ rubbed Stormy's neck. "She is so soft. What color do you think she'll be?"

"Chestnut, I think. See that red tinge? And her mane hasn't any dark hairs. She's a show-off, too, so I'll bet she's going to love the limelight. Some horses get a kick out of showing and others just tolerate it." Brad stroked the mare's neck. "We have an all-Arab show coming up in May. You want to enter her?"

"Where is it?"

"Up here. Not a big one. You could jump Herndon and show him in equitation. Give you a chance to show a horse you don't know well. I have a feeling someday you're going to be doing a lot of that, so you might as well get the experience."

The offhand way he spoke made DJ realize this meant a lot to him. "I'll ask Mom. It shouldn't be a problem."

"You know what we could do—bring Major when you come up here so you and Jackie can work with him, too. She's a good coach, even though she'd rather do dressage than jump."

DJ looked up from rubbing her cheek on Stormy's mane. Once the little filly decided to give in, she didn't mind being handled and leaned into the stroking. "She helped me a lot with the dressage. Major and I can always use more of that." She could hardly believe she said that, after all her heel digging about dressage. Jackie and Bridget had been right. Both she and Major were better athletes because of it.

Brad pulled a soft brush from his back pocket and handed it to DJ. "She loves this."

"You ready to go again?" Jackie stopped at the stall. "Herndon's waiting for you."

"Sure." DJ gave the baby one more pat and let herself out of the stall. "Bye, Stormy. You be good, now."

Stormy shook her head, sending her mane flopping from side to side. She twitched her tail and yawned.

"Sorry I bored you." DJ caught herself yawning, too. When Brad and Jackie followed suit, they all laughed.

"You two go on, and after I get a couple of things done, I'll saddle up Matadorian and we can ride along the river." He winked at DJ. "You'll need a break by then."

Putting Herndon through his dressage paces was like flying.

"You've learned a lot since the first time you rode him," Jackie said with a smile. "Feel what it's like when he bends around your leg. That way you'll know how it should feel for Major. The deeper you sit in that saddle, the more contact you have with him and the better you can drive him on the bit. Balance is everything in dressage, and it's the same in jumping."

She tapped DJ on the knee. "Don't look so serious. You're supposed to be having fun."

"I am. I just have to concentrate so hard to remember it all."

"Some of it is already second nature to you. I can tell you've been working hard."

I would have been further ahead if I hadn't been grounded for the last six months. DJ knew it hadn't really been that long, but it sure seemed like it.

"Now what?"

"N-nothing." *What? Is my face like an open book anyone can read?*

"If you have any questions, remember that the only dumb question is the one you don't ask."

"Thanks." DJ signaled Herndon forward again. "This

time we are going to do this perfect, you hear me?" The big horse's ears twitched back and forth as he listened to DJ and paid attention to everything going on around him, even the birds twittering in the rafters overhead.

"Relax, DJ," Jackie called.

"Relax, use your seat, more leg, keep your hands steady." DJ shook her head and Herndon faltered. "Fiddle. Do you have to be so sensitive?" She sucked in a deep breath and dropped her shoulders. *Right, relax. How come I get so tired trying to relax?*

"Come on, DJ, you're trying too hard. Let's have a simple canter, staying in half the ring. If you put a smile on your face, your shoulders will relax, and he'll come down on the bit."

Sure, add smile. DJ kept up a running inner monologue, but what Jackie said was true. When she smiled and relaxed, she sat deeper. With that, combined with her legs and holding the reins, she could feel Herndon come down. A smile, enjoy. She wasn't riding the Olympics yet, after all.

And you can bet you'll have to be relaxed then.

When Brad rode Matadorian into the ring, DJ was more than ready for a break. Both she and Herndon were sweating, and it wasn't because the sun was shining on them.

The next few days were repeats of the first one, with DJ dividing her time between Stormy and learning more about showing and working with Herndon both on dressage and jumping. The tall bay loved flying over jumps as much as she did. But unlike Major, who would try whatever she wanted, Herndon made her work for each jump.

If she faltered, he faltered. They had one bad takeoff, and DJ ended up on his neck.

"That was close." Jackie stroked Herndon's sweaty neck and looked up at DJ.

Her heart was still pounding like a runaway drum.

"So what did you do wrong? Or not do right?"

DJ thought. "I was behind, not up and over him enough."

"Good thing you have good balance, huh?" Jackie patted her knee.

Saturday afternoon DJ played with all the babies out in the pasture. They gathered around her for treats and raced her across the pasture. They quickly learned that she hid treats in her pockets and nosed her jacket after she said "no more." Smart horses that they were, they knew there were usually more.

"Hey, have you heard about Monty Roberts, the man who listens to horses?" Brad asked on the way home from church on Sunday morning.

"No, what about him?"

"He wrote a book called *The Man Who Listens to Horses*. He has a pretty different way of breaking horses and says he can break any horse and be riding it within half an hour. He's been all over the world teaching people about it. You want to go to one of his clinics sometime? He lives down in southern California."

"Sure. What does he do different?"

"He watches the horse's body language for "joining up" signals, for one thing. He's always gentle."

"Sounds cool."

"I'll give you my copy of his book." He winked at her. "You can use it for a book report. Kill two birds with one stone."

"Bradly Atwood, that's a terrible analogy to use." Jackie

loved birds and had feeders all around their house.

"Sorry." Brad looked at DJ in the rearview mirror. "You need to attend every clinic you can find if you're going for A levels."

"Not necessarily," Jackie disagreed with a smile. "You have an excellent trainer in Bridget, so the clinics are like the pickle on a hamburger. The better the pickle, the better the burger, but the meat is still the same."

"So what part are you?" DJ grinned and cocked her head.

"I'm the bun, and she's the cheese," Brad offered.

Even with their teasing, DJ felt like she was being sucked under by a huge wave. She'd be going home to a new house, all this training Brad was talking about, shows back to back . . . And what was her mother going to say about all this?

"What's wrong?" Jackie asked.

"Nothing." DJ made herself sit up straight and smile. "Nothing at all."

Liar, her little voice shrieked in her ear.

7

"I THINK IT'S TIME FOR A FAMILY MEETING."

DJ looked up from packing her duffel. Brad lounged against the doorframe of the room that had come to be her own. "What do you mean?"

"Well, the way it appears to me, you have more family now than you know what to do with. And most of them have no idea what it's going to take to help you get where you want to go."

"Me neither," she muttered as she rolled a sweat shirt and stuck it in the side.

"And at this point in your life, you don't even know if you have what it takes to be an Olympic rider."

"Gran says you can do anything if you want to bad enough and work hard for it." She stood upright. "And I do both."

"Deej, I know you do, and that's not what I'm talking about. I'm sure Bridget—in fact, I think she should be in on this meeting—has talked about her life in world competition. The stresses and expense and all."

"Nope, she hasn't. Not to us kids, anyway. She believes in the—what do you call it?" DJ wrinkled her nose to help her think better. "Oh, the need-to-know principle. She's a pretty private person."

"Ummm." Brad nodded with a faraway look in his eye. "Guess I better get to know Bridget better, too." He studied DJ through slightly closed eyes.

"What?"

"Just thinking. I know it is important to take one day at a time, but long-range planning is more valuable than you know."

"No, it's not. I mean, I know that. I've been planning on jumping in the Olympics for the last three years. I knew I had to learn to ride and I did. I had to get a horse and I did. And now I'm learning to jump and ride dressage. Right on track for my long-range plans."

"You're right. Come on, let's get you home before your mother comes looking for you. How does next weekend sound for this major meeting?"

She grabbed her duffel and her drawing case. "Nope. I'll be at the art thing in San Francisco, and Gran and Joe will be in New York for the award ceremony. Did I tell you she got an award for her artwork? Contributions to children's literature, they call it. She wanted me to go along since I helped her on the foal in that book."

"Darla Jean Randall, you are one mighty talented young lady. You have no idea how proud I am to know you." Brad took her duffel and slung his other arm over her shoulders.

"Is Jackie coming?"

"She'd better be since we're stopping in Sonoma for dinner on the way. How does Mexican sound?"

"Good. Can we stop and get some of that cheese?"

"Sonoma Jack?"

"Yeah, Mom really likes that. Especially the pesto one."

The closer she got to home, the quieter DJ grew.

"Hey, you sleeping back there?" Brad reached over the seat and patted her knee.

"No."

"So what's going through that blond head of yours?"

"Now, we'll have no blond jokes." Jackie looked over her shoulder. "Right, DJ?"

"Uh-huh." Her fingernails screamed to be trimmed—with her teeth. One was so rough it snagged on her sweater.

"You want to talk?" Brad's voice turned serious. "We can stop in Vallejo and get a Coke or something."

Do I want to talk? How do I know? What's wrong with me, anyway? Had a great time, and now I don't want to go home.

Brad swung into a fast-food place and ordered three drinks, then parked the car. He and Jackie both turned in their seats so they could see DJ.

"So what did Lindy say when you talked with her?"

"Oh . . . the move went well, they like the new house, that kind of stuff."

"You think that might have anything to do with the way you're feeling?"

"Why?" DJ sipped her drink.

"Well, they say that moving rates right up there near the top of the stress scale, along with fear of dying and public speaking."

"But I wasn't even there. The movers did the whole thing."

"Do you like the new house?"

"I guess; what's not to like?"

"Sometimes just the change is hard," Jackie added. "I'd be kind of concerned if it were me."

"Mom says I should be thrilled to have such a neat room. And we'll all have plenty of space and . . ." *And I want to go back to my own room and the yard Gran and I made and—-and I just want to go back.* She knew she meant back before her mother got married and back before Gran got married, back to the way things used to be. But that was crazy. Then she wouldn't have Major or Joe or Brad and Jackie and . . .

"Things just get all messed up."

"Yeah, life's like that. It'll probably get worse."

"What a big help you are." Jackie pushed Brad's arm off the back of the seat.

"How's the algebra coming?"

"Not to change the subject or anything." Jackie shook her head at Brad. "You keep it up and DJ will probably never come back."

"Fat chance." DJ felt her hands relax. "I think I'm beginning to get it, the algebra, I mean. Robert's a good coach, and like Amy said, I gotta quit saying 'I can't do algebra.' So now I always say 'I can do algebra,' and I'm trying to give it the same focus I do riding."

"Wow, that's a major step forward."

"I don't always make it."

"No, but it looks to me like you hit it right on the head. Some coach once told his team, 'If you think you can or you think you can't, you're right.' Makes a lot of sense when you think about it."

"Bridget never lets us say 'try' or 'I can't.' Man, you want to see her go ballistic, just say 'I can't.' She comes off the wall."

"Bridget? That cool-as-a-cucumber blond dynamo I met?"

"Well, you might not see it so much as hear it. Only an idiot would do it twice. No excuses, either—just own up to yes or no."

"Sounds to me like that woman is the perfect coach for you." Jackie sent DJ a special smile. "I wish I'd had someone like that when I was beginning. It keeps you from developing a heap of bad habits."

"You ready to go home now?" Brad set his empty drink container on the floor.

"I guess." And amazingly, she was.

But when they stopped at the new house instead of driving up to the old one, she had a hard time making herself open the door. "You want to come in?"

Brad and Jackie swapped looks, then Jackie said, "I think we'll pass this time. Your mother probably has enough on her hands with the move and all. We'll come see the new house later."

DJ climbed out, hauling her stuff with her. With her duffel and drawing kit in one hand, she reached back in for her boots. "Thanks for everything."

Brad got out and gave her a hug. "Hang in there, kid. You're going to make it."

"Thanks." She started to walk away.

"And, Deej, remember, if you need to talk, we're just a phone call away."

"'Kay."

Lights nestled in among the plants lining the walk up to the front door. Last time she'd been here, there'd been no lights, no plants, and come to think of it, the sidewalk curved now instead of lying straight. She took the three steps up to the porch slowly, each feeling more like a mountain than the one before. The double-wide front doors looked big enough to front a church. It was so quiet. Was anyone even home?

She turned the knob. When the door opened, she waved at Brad. He honked and backed out of the drive. DJ didn't even have a key in case they'd been gone.

Now she knew what going through a time warp must feel like. The chandelier in the entry reflected in the marble floor, but like the sunken living room off to the right, the space was empty. The stairs to the "children's wing," as her mother called it, curved up to the left, and an open walkway led to the new wing. The vaulted ceilings made her think she should whisper, like in church.

The temptation to just go on up to her room, if she could find the way, pulled her toward the stairs. But instead, she set her things down and followed the sound of voices to the kitchen, dining, family room, all in one.

Whatever did they need all this space for, anyway?

"Hi, I'm ho—here."

"DeeJay!" The twins leaped up from their old familiar sofa and pelted across the room, Velcroing themselves to her legs.

"We missed you."

"You was gone too long."

"Did you see your room?"

"Our room is this big." Arms stretched wide. Her right leg got a chance to breathe.

"Okay, guys, back off. Give DJ a chance to catch up."

She patted each of the blond heads and disentangled her legs. The boys rolled on the floor, so she gave each of them a tickle, then crossed to the marble counter and laid a sack on it. "For you, Mom. Well, for everyone, but . . ."

Lindy opened it up. "Oh, cheese. Sonoma Jack cheese with pesto. Right from Sonoma."

"I got the funny ends out of the barrel. You get more that way."

"Let's have some. There must be crackers here somewhere." Robert started slamming cupboard doors.

"Thanks, DJ." Her mother came around the counter to kiss DJ's cheek. "Over there, in that one." She pointed to a cupboard by the stainless-steel double-door refrigerator.

"Mommy, we want cheese."

"Yes, darlings, in a minute." She turned back to DJ. "There's sparkling cider in the refrigerator. You want to get that out? We've been waiting for you so we could celebrate moving into our new house. Cheese was the perfect thing to bring. Oh, and there's a tray of sliced apples and pears, too." She reached up into another cupboard and brought down the wine glasses. "Here, Robert, pour it into these."

He popped the cork just like a champagne bottle and poured the fizzing liquid into the glasses. "Okay, now, everyone—no, guys, you don't drink it yet—we're going to make a toast."

"Toast?"

"We's drinking juice, not toast."

"Just hold your glasses up like this, okay?" Robert demonstrated.

The boys giggled and did as told.

Standing next to her mother, DJ followed suit.

"To our new home. May Jesus Christ bless us here and dwell within our home and in our hearts." Robert touched his glass to Lindy's, then DJ's and the boys'. Once all the glasses touched, they drank to their new home.

They didn't even ask how my week went. DJ set her glass in the sink and helped herself to the cheese and crackers. *At least I did one thing right by bringing home the cheese.*

"Your bed's all made up and everything," Lindy said after mopping up a spill on the counter. "I told them to just leave the boxes—that you'd unpack them later."

"Okay. Did anyone call for me?"

"Oh yes, Amy and Mrs. Johnson." Lindy glanced at the clock. "It's not too late to return the calls. Thanks to Robert, you have a private phone line in your room." Lindy's rolled eyes gave her opinion on that.

"A private phone? Me?" When she looked at Robert, he nodded.

"You're a young lady now, and I thought you might like that, even though you aren't a phone hog."

"Thanks."

"Gran says she plans to take you shopping for art supplies. She about went nuts when she saw the wall of built-ins for your drawing things. I got dibs on buying the easel. We can set the spotlights for wherever you want them." He stopped a moment. "Would you mind if we made a big copy of your Stormy drawing and hung it over the fireplace?" He pointed to the blank area above the mantel. Bookshelves lined the walls on either side of the fieldstone fireplace. A fire crackled even though it wasn't really cold enough to need the heat.

DJ went to stand in front of it. She looked up at the wall. "I guess. Are you sure that's what you want there?"

Robert came to stand beside her. "We'll have it matted and framed. Unless there is another picture of yours you like better?"

"No, I can't . . . I just . . ."

"Spit it out."

"Well, you've been looking at decorator stuff, and that's . . . I mean . . . well, I'm just a kid and not a great artist."

"Yet." He laid an arm across her shoulders and drew her into his side. "Nothing would please me more than to hang one of your early drawings there. Someday we can say 'We knew her when . . .' "

DJ looked up to see him smiling down at her. "You really mean that, don't you?"

"Just wait and see how fast we can get it done. You want to help pick out the frame? I saw one that had weathered-looking wood and some leather. Seemed to be begging to frame a horse."

"Thanks." The warm glow that rose from her toes clear to the top of her hair had nothing to do with the blazing fire. How come one second she could feel like a block of ice and the next be like a bud blossoming in springtime? This up-and-down stuff was getting to be a drag.

"DJ, come see your room."

"See ours, too."

So much for the warm moment. She let the twins pull

her by the hands, through the arched door and up the stairs. They chattered nonstop until Robert, who followed close behind, clapped a hand over one mouth.

"Remember, that's supposed to be a surprise."

Good thing she hadn't been really listening.

Bobby or Billy, one or the other, pushed open the door to her room and the other pulled her in.

Her room glowed in the desert colors taken from a horse picture by a famous southwest artist. The framed print took up a good part of the wall above her bed. Even the comforter on the bed swirled like a desert sunset. Bookshelves, cubbyholes, slots for canvas or poster board, thin drawers, deep drawers, and doors all covered one entire wall. She had as much storage space as the art room at school, and this was arranged better. Her poster of the horse jumping through the five Olympic rings held the place of honor between the windows on the south wall.

"Don't you like it, DJ?"

"You don't say nothing."

DJ squatted down between the two boys. "I don't know what to say."

"You could say it's pretty."

"I think it's pretty."

"Oh man, so do I." She ruffled their hair and stood up to give first Robert, then her mother a hug. "Thank you."

"Gran and I helped the decorator. Gran knew you liked this artist."

"But you said . . . the boxes . . ."

"I know." Lindy giggled and put an arm around DJ's waist. Robert did the same from the other side. "We wanted to surprise you."

"You did." DJ nodded, then shook her head. "You sure did." She hugged both her parents at the same time. When they hugged her back, she felt like the middle of a sandwich. Gran and Joe sometimes gave her the same feeling.

"See your 'puter." One of the double Bs pulled her to the desk that had been half hidden by the open door. "We gots one, too."

"Only yours is bigger."

Her school books were lined up on the shelf above the computer and monitor, along with a dictionary and some other reference books. The shelf above that held her model horse collection and a framed photograph of Major that said *Love, from Amy*.

DJ turned to her mom. "Are you sure this is all for me, that you didn't adopt someone else while I was gone?"

"Yes, we're sure. That's why it seemed so perfect when you were going to Brad's at moving time."

"We really did want to surprise you. This gave us extra time to finish." Robert sat down on the bed. "There's a trundle under here for when you want to have someone sleep over."

"Has Amy seen this?" DJ swept the room with her arm.

"Sure did. She brought you that picture for her room-warming gift."

"They were going somewhere tonight, or she'd have been here waiting."

DJ walked around the room, touching the paper slots, opening a drawer, checking out the closet. Her clothes hung neatly in place, as if she'd left them only moments before.

"See the bathroom."

"And the 'cuzzi tub. It makes noise."

"And bubbles."

DJ fell asleep that night with guilt on her mind. And she'd been wondering if her family really cared. "God, I sure messed up again, didn't I?" Was that a heavenly chuckle she heard or merely the wind in the trees outside?

Her week passed in a blur. Monday she got eighty percent on her algebra quiz, her best grade ever. Major was no longer limping, hadn't been for four days. So she got to ride him, nice and easy but a good workout.

Tuesday her three girls welcomed Andrew back into their class and made him laugh till he forgot to be afraid. Wednesday Gran and Joe left for New York. Thursday she got to take a dressage lesson. She still hesitated to jump Major, but she could tell he felt good.

Friday she left school early so the entire family could take her into San Francisco for her art weekend. They stopped in front of a three-story Victorian mansion with the trim painted in white and three shades of purple.

"It's huge." DJ gulped. And here she'd been wondering how there would be room enough for ten kids.

"It probably has a basement, too," Robert said, shaking his head. "How I would love to have one of these old ladies to renovate."

"I do hope you mean the house," Lindy said. She snagged a hand of each of the boys, who were on their way to check out the wrought-iron fence.

"Funny." Robert turned to DJ. "You got everything?" At her nod, he dug his wallet out of his back pocket and handed her a twenty-dollar bill. "I know the paper says all your expenses are taken care of, but you might need some money."

"But Mom already gave me—"

"That's fine. This is just to be sure."

DJ took the money and put it in her backpack along with the ten from Lindy. She took in a deep breath. "Guess I better go up there." The ancient concrete stairs from the street up had moss and a fern growing out of the cracks. A fuschia so old its gnarly trunk was thicker than her wrist dropped pink and purple petals, like drooping dancing ladies, on the lichen-covered rocks and gray stairs.

"I'll go with you and make sure we're in the right place."
Robert took her duffel bag and started up the steps.

Looking up at a round stained-glass window in a dormer on the third floor, DJ shook her head. What was she getting into now? And what she wouldn't give to be back at the barns!

8

DJ KNEW SHE WAS IN LOVE.

And it had nothing to do with guys.

The way Isabella Gant used her pencils and charcoals to create her drawings was nothing short of miraculous in DJ's eyes. She watched carefully as the artist used overheads and slides to show the progression of strokes. While she already understood some about the value of lines, now it made even more sense. And never before had she heard of negative space.

By Saturday afternoon she was looking at the world through entirely new eyes.

She hated to take breaks, wanting to learn every bit that she could. But talking with other kids who loved to draw was fun, too. So was walking the hills of San Francisco with a sketch pad in hand.

Sunday morning they were sent out two by two with instructions to bring back three drawings, each one with a different purpose.

Paired with redheaded Sean Maclaine, she raced him down the long steps from Broadway to the marina district. Sun and a good breeze brought San Francisco Bay alive with sailboats running before the wind over swells deep enough to send spume flying over the bows. Golden Gate

Bridge arched high above the bay waters, for once not hidden by the fog that hung out on the horizon.

"Do you sail?" Sean asked, pausing to point out a double-masted catamaran with full sails flying.

"No. Not unless you call taking a horse over jumps sailing. We sail through the air, not water." DJ pulled out her pad to do her six-line sketch of a pot with tulips. "Do you?"

"Some. I crew for a local boat during the races sometimes."

"Really?" DJ flipped the paper over and tried again. Sean, too, was sketching away.

DJ looked down the length of steps. They'd stopped on the halfway landing. Primroses, pansies, and tulips lined the concrete steps, along with some flowering shrubs she didn't recognize. Late-blooming pink and white camellias colored the shade from the eucalyptus trees bordering the Presidio, an army base in existence since the early settlement days of San Francisco.

If only she could capture color with pencils. One of these days she'd be taking oils and acrylics in art class. She had worked some with pastels, but her fingers seemed to like pencil best. For now.

When they got to the bottom of the stairs, they jogged the remaining blocks to the Palace of Fine Arts, a monument left from the San Francisco World Fair in 1939. A path circled the pond inhabited by ducks and geese along with several pairs of swans. DJ stopped to sketch a turtle dozing in the shade of drooping grasses.

So many things to draw. She set to work, filling one page after another.

"We have half an hour before we have to start back."

"Already?" She looked up and caught the shadows of the domed building with arches. "Just a few more minutes."

She sketched with all the speed she could muster, getting the main lines down and hoping she would remember what to fill in later.

Sean stretched and DJ sketched the angle of his arm. He had an easy-to-draw face with a strong square jaw and straight nose. Copper hair flopped over one eyebrow, and a diamond stud twinkled in his earlobe.

While she drew him, he drew her.

"Two minutes. You think we can run those stairs in two minutes?"

DJ slung her things into her backpack and shoved both arms in the straps. "Not if we sit here any longer." Off they went, pounding along the sidewalk.

"You're in . . . good . . . shape."

"You . . . too." They stopped halfway up the stairs to get their breath.

"We're . . . late." Puff, pant.

"Then . . . what . . . are we . . . waiting . . . for?"

DJ's legs shook so badly she could barely lift them over the last step. And they still had a block to go. Other kids from the group were straggling in same as they were.

Ms. Gant met them at the door. "So you found things to draw?" She looked at her watch. "But you are late. I think there is no time for lunch." At their groans, she laughed, a full-bodied laugh that invited them all to join in. "Come, Ramona has lunch on the table. We will talk while we eat."

DJ's drawing of the turtle was pinned up as a good example of light and shadow. It seemed she could draw more than just horses after all.

"I hope you will continue to draw," Ms. Gant said as DJ put her things away after the final session on Sunday afternoon. "You have an unusual talent for someone your age for getting a feeling across in your pictures. Many people spend a lifetime trying to learn that."

DJ swallowed. "Th-thank you. I really loved being here—with you." She followed the other students as they left, all of them saying their good-byes.

Sean met her at the door. "It was fun working with you. I'd like to go drawing with you again. I live in Palo Alto, you know, but I can drive."

"I have a horse show at the Palo Alto Equestrian Center in June. You could come to that if you like." She shrugged. "Not that I'll have time to draw, but you could."

"Good. I'll bring my sketch pad." He stopped, looked at his feet, then at her. "Could I have your phone number? We had fun talking."

DJ could feel the heat climbing from her chest to the roots of her hair. "I . . . I guess." She gave him her home phone, then laughed. "I got a private line in our new house, but I don't even know my own number."

Sean laughed, too. "See ya." He ran down the steps to where a Mercedes waited at the street and turned to wave. "Bye, DJ. Keep on drawing."

Wait till Gran hears about all this, DJ thought as she walked down the stairs when her family drove up. She talked nonstop all the way home.

"I think she had a good time," Robert said when they turned in the drive.

"What was your first clue?" Lindy asked, then caught herself on a yawn. "I think all this moving is catching up with me."

"Aren't you glad you don't have to go into the office in the morning?" Robert propped his arms on the steering wheel. "I sure am."

"Me too." DJ caught herself in surprise. She was glad. Her mother seemed more relaxed, and the frown lines between her eyebrows weren't so noticeable.

"Daddy, I hafta go to the bathroom."

"Me too."

Robert groaned. "All right, so much for kicking back a minute."

"Daddy, you can kick up when we get in the house."

DJ snorted as she reached in the back for her duffel and her bulging art carrier. *Kick up. What funny guys.*

"You going to show me your drawings?" Lindy sat with the car door open and her feet on the ground. She sniffed the air. "You smell that?"

DJ sniffed, too. Something was blooming, that was for sure. The fragrance perfumed the air all around them. "They might not mean much without having heard the instructions."

"That's okay. I just like to see what you do."

Together the two of them strolled up the curving walk to the front door. Robert leaned against the doorjamb. "My two favorite women. What a picture you make."

They headed straight for the kitchen, where DJ spread her work out on the counter for her mother to see. As soon as Robert finished giving each of the boys a string cheese stick, he joined them.

DJ pointed out which were the beginning ones and which were the last.

"I'd say you learned a lot." Robert picked up the turtle picture and tapped the paper. "Any chance I could have this one?"

"It's not done yet."

"Okay, when you finish."

"Sure, but what for?"

"I'd like to frame it and keep it in my office. Makes me relax just looking at it. I can feel the sun on my back and . . ."

Lindy yawned again. "Look at me. You say the word *relax* and I yawn." She gave DJ a one-arm hug. "I think the sun got to me. I'm going to lie down for a while. Don't let me sleep long." She stopped at the doorway. "Darla Jean, I am real proud of you. Not only the drawing but you in general."

"Thanks, Mom."

"That goes double for me." Robert helped her gather her drawings up to put in her canvas portfolio case. "You know, I've been thinking."

"Now what?"

"You might consider an art class at Mount Diablo College this summer or one of the classes in the city. Maybe Ms. Gant offers some." He leaned back against the counter and crossed both his arms and his legs. "If you don't have to work so hard for money at the Academy, you might have time for that. Besides, you've had money-making schemes in the past."

DJ kept a straight face with great difficulty as she remembered the loose critters in the garage and Lindy's great dislike for them. "You weren't thinking of getting the boys hamsters or mice, were you?"

"Not a chance."

"Good thing."

They shared a grin at her mother's expense.

"I do plan on a dog or two, though."

"Cool."

"You have any requests?"

"Other than horses?"

"You got that right. I've got Bridget looking for either two POAs, or she suggested a Welsh pony or cross."

"Ponies of America are small horses, so they're not as stubborn as Shetlands. They'd be cool." She raised an eyebrow. "I always wanted a Newfoundland puppy."

"Then we won't need two horses. The dog can fill in. DJ, those things get monstrous. You got time to take it to an obedience class?"

"Well, you asked."

"I was thinking more along the line of a golden re-

triever or Lab. Your mother suggested a Jack Russell ter-
rier because they like to play so much. Smart little dogs,
too."

"Just so we don't get a yappy dog. I hate that."

"Me too."

DJ cocked one eyebrow. "How about a boa constrictor?
I have a friend who has one, says they're really full of personality and friendly."

"That the guy who took the runaway hamsters?"

"Uh-huh."

"You don't really want a snake for a pet."

"Should we ask Mom?"

"You want to keep your head?"

The boys charged in.

"You guys ever think of walking in the house?"

"We's in a hurry." Bobby grabbed DJ's hand.

"We *are* in a hurry," Robert corrected.

"We are? Where we going?" The two began dancing in
place.

Robert groaned. "Come on, let's go read a story."

DJ laughed at the look of defeat on Robert's face. He let
the boys drag him over to the bookshelf, sending DJ a help-
me look. She ignored him. "Have fun, guys. I've got homework to do."

But before she hit the books, she called Amy on her new
phone and told her all about the weekend.

When DJ slowed down, Amy said, "I got the cards
from the printshop. When can we put the packets together?"

"Tomorrow night, depending on how much homework
I have." DJ made a face at the stack of books on her desk.
She'd been caught up on Thursday, but not now. Why did
teachers give extra over the weekends? Didn't they want
kids to have any kind of life outside of school?

"I'm done."

"Good, come and do mine."

When they hung up, DJ sighed and started with her journal. She had plenty to write in that. The ringing phone made her jump. She wasn't used to having a phone in her room yet.

"So how was the art class?" Brad's voice sounded extra deep.

"Great." By the time she told him everything, another half hour had flown by. She glanced at her portfolio case. If only she had time to work some more on a couple of the drawings.

And if only she had six or ten more hours in a day. Since she hadn't gotten a lot of sleep in San Francisco, her eyes felt as though someone had thrown a handful of sand in her face. Maybe a short nap would help.

She got up and stretched, went in the bathroom, and splashed cold water on her face. If she lay down now, she'd never get up until morning. If then.

When her chin bumped the top of her desk, she gave up. She must have read the same page in history five times and still had no idea whether they were talking about a war or a dance.

By Monday night DJ was sure she was caught in a blender with the lid on tight.

She didn't have to work Patches, so she should have had plenty of extra time. But putting the note packets together took up three hours, and they weren't completely done— there were just enough to send to the shop in Connecticut that her aunt Julia's friend owned and some for the tack shop at the Academy. They also matted some of the prints of Stormy, leaving others plain.

"No, you guys go on. We're busy." DJ shooed the boys away for the third time.

"You girls ready for dinner?" Lindy called from the kitchen.

"In a minute." DJ taped the box for the gift shop and Amy applied the label.

"Did you put the invoice in?" Amy glanced around the long table they had set up to work on in the empty living room.

"I think so." DJ picked up a stack of prints—and groaned. "No, it's right here."

"We'll send it in a separate envelope, then. No biggy."

"You think we'll ever sell this many?" DJ motioned to the remaining box of cards.

"Just you watch. Next time we'll have to print double this amount."

"Let's eat and then stuff some more. I have to work on my term paper, and if you say you have yours done already, I may have to stomp all over you."

"Nope, but I do have the research done and I've started the writing."

"Wish I could hire you to do mine."

"You couldn't pay me enough, even if it weren't cheating."

"Robert's stuck in traffic, so we'll eat without him." Lindy set the platter of sliced meat loaf in the middle of the table. "There, let's have grace. Bobby," she nodded to the boy on DJ's right, "will you say grace?"

"I'm Billy."

Lindy groaned. DJ snickered to herself. She'd known that.

"Just say grace."

"Come Lord Jesus . . ." For a change he didn't ask Jesus to bless everyone he knew, naming each and anything else he could think until the food got cold.

"You girls go on and finish what you were doing. The boys and I will clean up," Lindy said after the apple crisp dessert had been devoured.

"Thanks, Mom." DJ and Amy headed back to the living room.

"How come you gripe all the time about how grouchy your mom is? I think she's cool."

"She's different now that she's not working." While DJ hadn't thought much about that, she realized how true it was. She hadn't been barked at in a week, but then, who was counting?

Tuesday night when Brad called to say *the* meeting was set up for Sunday afternoon, she had to swallow twice before she could answer. "B-but I planned to ride up in Briones if the weather's okay."

"I think this is more important, don't you?"

Maybe to you, but I haven't been up in the park for weeks. First it was storming, then I was on restrictions, and since then I haven't even had time to blow my nose.

"DJ?"

"I'm here. I'll see you on Sunday, then." She stormed down to the kitchen. "Why didn't you tell me you'd talked to Brad?"

Lindy's eyebrows hit her hairline. "I have to tell you all my phone calls now?"

"No! Just that one." DJ locked her arms across her chest.

"You don't want us to get together?"

"No, it's not that. I . . . Joe and I have that jumping clinic in Sacramento on Saturday. And on Sunday I was hoping to go riding and . . ."

Her mother's eyes narrowed. "Make up your mind, Darla Jean. You want us to support you, but on your terms, is that it?"

"No, but . . ." Why did she feel like crying? She swallowed hard. She started to say "I just never have any time for my stuff" but stopped that by coughing.

With her mother watching her, DJ felt like a mouse must when a cat has it by the tail and is playing with it.

"It's not easy, you know, trying to schedule something with so many people. That was the only time Robert and Bridget had available. Gran and Joe think this is so important that they turned down a dinner invitation with some friends, and *you* would rather go riding up in Briones?"

DJ sniffed. Put like that, she sounded like the most selfish, babyish brat in the country. "Sorry." She turned on her heel and headed back to her room. The room that felt too big and too fancy and too . . . Just like the rest of the house. Just like the rest of . . . She threw herself across the fancy comforter that wasn't much comfort at all. Her old one, the one Gran had made for her, absorbed tears much better.

What was the matter with her?

Even Thursday evening spent listening to Gran and Joe's adventures in New York made her feel good only for a little while. Gran's trophy was awesome, and the huge framed picture of her book cover was glorious. So why'd she feel like crying—again!

Friday morning she found out. Three zits and her period.

"You going to have PMS like your mother?" She glared at the pimply face in the bathroom mirror. "Fiddle and double fiddle." She scrubbed her face raw. Her hair stuck out all over and wouldn't be tamed. "My period, zits, and a bad hair day. What else can go wrong?"

"My, aren't we Miss Cheerful this morning." Lindy turned from scrambling eggs. "Slamming doors won't make things better."

Neither will kicking walls, but that's what I feel like doing. "I'm not hungry."

"Eat anyway." Lindy set the plate on the table and pointed at the chair.

DJ slumped in the seat and glared at the pale yellow pile of guck on her plate. Her mother had even put bacon in it, one of DJ's favorite breakfast foods. And melted cheese on top. She looked up at her mother's stern face and took a forkful of eggs. Halfway to her mouth, some fell off and bounced from her shirt to the floor, leaving a grease stain on its way.

If DJ were a cussing person, this was the time for it.

"Fiddle!" she said—and thought worse.

"Darla Jean Randall, what's the matter with you?" Lindy glared at her daughter. Suddenly her face relaxed. "Ah, the PMS bug has bit."

DJ swallowed her bite of scrambled eggs. "Yes! And it's all your fault. I'm just like you!"

A car horn honked. She scooped up the last bite and stuck the remaining corner of toast between her lips. Snagging her jacket and backpack off the chair knob, she headed for the front door, her mother still laughing behind her.

"Hope you're feeling better by the time you come home, Miss Merry Sunshine," Lindy called after her. The boys shouted their good-byes, and DJ escaped out the door.

9

HOW COULD SHE BE HEARING the alarm when she'd just closed her eyes?

"DJ." A tap on her door.

"Yes?"

"Are you up? You're supposed to be over at the Academy in ten minutes. Didn't your alarm go off?"

DJ groaned. She did remember it ringing. Did she smack the Off button instead of Snooze?

The jumping clinic!

Her feet hit the floor before her eyes finished opening. "Thanks, Robert. I'll be ready in a couple of minutes. Isn't Joe picking me up here?"

"He called and asked me to bring you to the Academy. Said he wanted an early start."

Finally the jumping clinic in Sacramento, and DJ had overslept. *How could you be so stupid!* DJ yelled inwardly. She pulled on her jeans and sweat shirt. So much for needing a shower. Thank the good Lord for hair long enough to wear in a ponytail. By the time she'd brushed her teeth and washed her face, the ten minutes were about up. She stuffed her supplies into her duffel bag, including her boots and helmet. A glance through the vertical blinds showed stars up above. Clear weather at least.

They would have about an hour and a half drive to Sacramento, and the clinic started at 8:30. No wonder Joe was up before the sun even thought about lightening the eastern horizon. Of course, she couldn't see the sunrise—not only did her room face west, but the high range of hills just east of them blocked much of the early dawn.

Robert handed her an apple, a food bar, and a juice box when she climbed in the front seat of the already running vehicle. "You need the nourishment. I'm sure Gran packed extra food for both you and Joe, but this is my contribution."

"Thanks. I can't believe I overslept."

"I'm glad Dad called, or we all would have been snoozing still."

DJ wanted nothing more than to tip her seat back and grab a few more Zs. Instead, she ate the food Robert handed her and tried to keep from breaking her jaw yawning. At least she and Joe were going alone to Sacramento so she could sleep. Joe wouldn't mind.

Bunny was leading her horse into the trailer beside Major when they drove into the Academy parking lot.

DJ groaned.

"Now what?" Robert looked to where she pointed. "So?"

"Forget it. Thanks for the ride. See you tonight." She opened the door, taking the last sip of the juice as her feet hit the gravel. Robert held out his hand, so she gave him the empty container. "Don't say I never gave you anything." She did manage to smile on that one.

"At least I get to go home and sleep awhile longer."

"With your luck, the twins will be up already."

Robert rolled his eyes and nodded. "I hope you're wrong. Have a good time."

DJ waved again and ambled to the trailer, where she could hear Bunny talking to her horse. Major nickered from his side of the silver-and-green rig.

"I thought I might have to come roll you out," Joe said, coming around the side of the trailer. "I think I have all of your equipment, but you better check."

"How come. . . ?" DJ whispered and nodded toward the trailer.

"She's having trouble with her truck. I offered."

"Oh." What could she say? Joe was just being Joe. But now there would be three of them in the cab and no chance to sleep. Besides, she liked the time with Joe—by herself. But another thought made her brighten. At least now he wouldn't be able to grill her on any of their unfinished discussions. He had a better memory than an elephant. And sometimes DJ just wanted to forget, especially when he cut to the quick, which was most of the time.

Within minutes they were on the road, with Bunny apologizing for intruding.

"Hey, it's not like we didn't have room or anything, is it, DJ?" Joe gave her a nudge with his elbow.

"Nope. No sense taking two rigs, anyway. If I'd known you were going, I'd have asked you along." She could feel her grandfather's approval right through her jacket. "Didn't you go last week?"

"Yes. That's why I registered for today, too. He was so good. If I learn as much again today as I did then, it'll be more than worth the time."

"I know *I'll* learn a lot."

Between watching other students and her turn with the trainer, DJ learned two really important things. Number one: She had so much to learn. And number two: All trainers were not the same. And having Bunny in the stands beside her helped her even more.

"So was that so bad?" Joe turned the ignition when they were ready to leave the Academy.

"No. How come Bunny could be so fun and funny today, but around the Academy she's always so serious?" DJ slid far enough down on her spine that she could prop her knees against the dashboard. "Nobody ever sees this side of her."

"People are strange. Maybe things are getting better for her."

"I guess."

"So are you looking forward to the *big* meeting tomorrow?"

DJ groaned. "Thanks for reminding me. Not to change the subject or anything, but do you think all that jumping bothered Major's shoulder any?"

"Why? Did you feel him act different?"

"No . . . yes . . . I'm not sure." She thought back to the jumps they'd taken and retaken. Had he been a bit hesitant? Or was it just that she'd been concentrating on Gray's instructions to the point of not paying as close attention to Major as usual?

"We'll watch him carefully for the next few days. You know, that clinic helped me today, too."

DJ shot him a sideways look. "How? You don't plan to start jumping Ranger now, do you?"

"No, nothing like that, but I guess I never quite realized how much goes into training a jumper. Or riding one." He shook his head. "Major has a lot to learn."

"Me too."

"Some guy sitting up behind me thought you did real well. Said if you had a decent horse, you'd go a long way."

"Decent horse! What kind of a jerk was he? Major took

every jump and never balked once." DJ's heels hit the floor-boards. "Good thing I didn't hear him, or I'd have—"

"Easy. You have to keep in mind that Major's just an old police horse. He wasn't born and bred for jumping like these big-time horses are."

"Major's got more heart than all of them put together. There never will be a more willing horse than him."

"Heart he has. Class he lacks." Joe patted her knee. "You've got to be realistic here, so quit sputtering."

"Major's the best horse any girl could have. . . ."

"Sure he is—in the beginning. People who compete out-grow their horses. Look at Jackie and Herndon."

DJ rolled her lips together. "Major's really special."

"He sure is, and so are you. Just trying to prepare you. See you tomorrow."

"Thanks for taking me. And taking notes." She waved the clipboard with his even handwriting covering several pages. "Bridget will be glad to see these, too." She waved again as he backed into the paved strip they used for a turn-around.

The thought of the mountain of homework that awaited her turned her feet to cement. Not that the stack was so high, just that her book report was due on Monday and she had half a book to go. She'd rather be reading *The Man Who Listens to Horses*, but since she'd already started this one, she figured she'd finish it. Besides, half of that one was much shorter than the whole of the other.

"So how did it go?" Robert asked. He glanced up at her but continued to wield his flashing chef's knife, turning carrots into skinny ovals.

"Good, I guess. My brain's still spinning." DJ snuck a couple of carrot slices. "That man has eyes better than an eagle's. And I thought Bridget was tough." She hung a hip on one of the stools by the green marble-topped counter. "What are you making?"

104

"Stew." Lindy turned from the stove, where she was browning the meat. "Bridget phoned a bit ago. Wanted you to call her at home if you got back later than six."

DJ glanced at the clock. 6:30. "Did she say what she wanted?"

"Nope. Dinner will be ready in about an hour."

Robert shook his head. "I'll never get used to these pressure cookers. Stew is supposed to simmer all afternoon." He started scrubbing potatoes.

"Then we couldn't have gone puppy hunting."

"Puppy hunting? Did you find one?" DJ snitched a couple more carrot pieces.

"Look, you eat all those up and you can cut more." Robert pointed the vegetable brush at her. "And the answer is maybe. We're thinking we should look at the Humane Society before we decide. Or check with ARF."

"That's the Animal Rescue Foundation," Lindy said at DJ's confused look.

"You mean we'd get a used dog?" DJ popped a carrot in her mouth.

"Darla Jean Randall, what a thing to say." But Lindy chuckled as she said it.

"Nope, recycled."

"Robert!"

"Just so it's not a hot dog." DJ slid off the stool, grabbed some more carrots, and fled the room, her mother's laughter chasing her out the door. She turned and stuck her head back around the wall. "Where are the boys? I knew things were too quiet here."

"Next door at the neighbors. Which reminds me, they're supposed to be home by dark."

DJ hustled up the stairs before her mother could suggest she go get them. Nice to know there were kids in the neighborhood for the boys to play with. That hadn't been the case at their other house.

Just thinking the words *other house* made her wish for the cozy family room and the bedroom that had been hers all her life. She pushed open the door to her new room. Sure it was beautiful—but it still wasn't the same. She dumped her stuff and headed for the bathroom. A shower would feel mighty good.

Call Bridget. DJ stopped at her desk and picked up the phone. Bridget answered on the first ring.

"Mom said you called."

"First, I want to thank you for taking Bunny along. Second, how was the clinic?"

DJ gave her a play-by-play account and finished with the stranger's comment about Major.

"He is right. But this year Major will be sufficient."

"Oh." DJ knew better than to argue with Bridget.

After hanging up the phone, she stopped in the bathroom doorway and eyed the Jacuzzi tub. She hadn't even had time to turn it on yet. "You can read and relax at the same time." She nodded at the face in the mirror. The one with a sunburned nose. Turning on the water, she hummed a tune as she retrieved her book and robe. She pinned up her hair, and when the tub was full enough, flipped the switch for the jets.

The tub roared into life, water swirling and burbling. Sinking down into the hot water with the jets sending pulses of water at her back, sides, and feet felt absolutely delicious. She trailed a hand past one of the jets, the bubbles massaging her fingers.

Maybe there were good things about this new house after all.

Except that she nearly fell asleep reading her book. She caught it just as the bottom edge hit the water.

"DJ, dinner's ready." Her mother knocked on the bathroom door and called at the same time. She stuck her head around the door. "Kind of nice, huh?"

"I'll say." DJ sat up and flipped the switch so the jets swooshed silent. "I'll be there in a couple of minutes, 'kay?"

"John Yamamoto is going to watch the boys," Lindy said the next afternoon as they got ready to head to Gran's for *the meeting*. "If you two want to walk over now, I'll come when he gets here. Mom might need some help with something."

Robert nodded. "You get the salad out of the fridge, and I'll bring the sack of chips and dips."

DJ did as he asked. How come right now she'd rather go hide out in the closet than go to *the meeting*? Talk about butterflies. Horse shows were nothing compared to this.

10

THEY TALKED ABOUT HER AS IF she were invisible.

"Yes," Bridget responded in answer to a question, "I believe DJ has the capabilities to become an Olympic rider, but there are many variables that can happen between now and then. One of the good things about the equestrian program is that age is not the governing principle as in other sports. DJ does not have to be a star by age sixteen. In fact, the chances of that happening are slim to none. Skill and experience both play such a strong part that there are many years of training and competing ahead of her—expensive years."

"And she has to have the right horses," Brad added.

"The right horses and the right sponsors. Many of the Olympic riders have corporate sponsors these days. But all of that is far in the future."

"I hate to show my ignorance, but what are those world-class horses running nowadays?" Robert cut to the bottom line.

"You don't really want to know." Joe shook his head. "Bunny and I were talking yesterday. It's six figures and up."

Maybe I should just slide down on the floor and slither out of here. Hey, guys, this is my life you're discussing. As soon as that thought surfaced, another kicked in. *Go ahead, be an ungrateful brat. They're trying to help you.*

She sat more firmly on her hands.

"So where do we go from here?" Robert asked.

"DJ is doing her best to learn all she can. Horses respond well to her. Patches is a good example of that. Few others could have brought him along as fast as she did."

DJ felt a glow all the way to her toenails. Bridget really thought *that*? And here she thought Patches was way behind.

"She is consistent, remembers what she has learned, and is learning more and more how to focus. And how to not tear herself down." Bridget looked around the group. "On the other hand, she is young and has not been exposed to the world of competitive showing. There are a lot of politics out there, and some dirty things going on, too."

"So you're saying she has to get more involved in the show world immediately." Robert glanced at Lindy. Her smile quivered, but she nodded.

"If this is what DJ really wants, then . . . then . . ." Lindy shook her head. "I have no idea how we are going to do all this."

"We are all going to do this together." Joe looked at Gran, and the two of them nodded, much like the twins did, as if a master puppeteer pulled the same strings.

"While Jackie and I aren't involved in the jumping world, we are out in the show-ring. And we have the next horse for DJ, as soon as she is ready."

"I . . . I'll be showing Major." DJ cleared her throat. When they nodded at her statement, she gained some more courage. "And I'm registered for that big show in two weeks. I can't start much sooner than that."

Jackie winked at her. "Just keep in mind that Herndon will be ready whenever you are. I've hired a jumping trainer for him since he was trained in dressage."

DJ gulped. Jackie said that so easily, as if hiring a trainer for a horse was no big deal at all.

"You know what? I think we'll bring him down to you when we can. Easier to bring the horse to the girl, though we'd rather you came to our house much more often," Jackie added.

"Something to keep in mind." Brad got their attention again. "Besides having horses of their own, the big players ride for a lot of people in all stages of training. That old thing about not keeping all your eggs in one basket is so true here."

"So for now, DJ can stay with Major. What else does she need immediately?"

"Two lessons jumping and one lesson in dressage every week—plus all the riding time she can get." Bridget looked at DJ. "Yes, she can and must stay with Major, if for no other reason than to prove she can. She also needs good grades so she can attend all the shows necessary."

"I'm working on that."

"And she needs to get up on as many horses as possible. Bunny said DJ can ride her horse sometimes."

"That's real nice of her," Joe said with a pleased smile. He looked down at Gran beside him. "She seems like a real nice lady."

DJ stared at the worn spot on her jeans. Why was Bunny doing this? She wanted to jump big-time herself. Her attitude surely had changed.

DJ looked over at Gran, who gave her a wise smile, the one that said "See, God knows what He is doing."

DJ realized she had missed something in the conversation. Something about a trust fund? Whatever that was. She'd have to ask Joe later.

"I would appreciate it if we could have a list of the possible horse shows to attend as soon as it is available. That way we can discuss this as a family and make plans." Lindy hadn't said much during all the discussion, but to DJ's ears, this sounded positive.

"Well, I think we are on the right track." Brad looked around the circle. "And I for one think we have been given an unprecedented opportunity here, to help a young woman go for her dreams and to be part of God's plan for her life, if this is what He indeed wants her to do."

"And that we'll learn through time and prayer. He's given Darla Jean many talents, and I expect He wants her to develop all of them, but maybe not all at the same time." Gran smiled again at DJ. "So I hope that all of us commit to praying daily for this child of ours and that she will commit to this, also."

DJ nodded along with the rest of them. Leave it to Gran to make sure all the plans were covered with prayer. DJ felt her head spinning. What if she really wasn't all that good? What if she let these people down? And herself? And God?

"DJ, all we expect of you is that you do your best." Joe drilled her with his interrogator eye. "Don't worry about any more than that. One day at a time." He paused. "And one more thing. You have to be willing to ask for help and let us know when you are feeling overwhelmed or confused or scared or whatever."

"Amen to that." Lindy's voice carried a load of feeling.

DJ sniffed. "I know." She forced a smile to her dry lips. "But you might have to remind me once in a while."

"Her and me both," Brad said under his breath.

"Anyone interested in dessert?" Gran got up from her chair. "Come on, Darla Jean, help me dish up."

After everyone had a piece of apple pie and a beverage, DJ stopped behind her chair before sitting down. "I . . . I have something to say."

Slowly the conversation died and all eyes turned toward her.

She shrugged and smiled a little smile. "Just thanks,

that's all. Thank you for coming, and thank you for wanting to help me. I'm a lucky kid." She slid into her chair to the "you're welcomes" from around the table.

"You done good, kiddo," Joe whispered when she went around the table later with the coffeepot, refilling cups.

After everyone left and she got home again, DJ settled into doing her homework. Talk about going from dreaming big dreams to reality. And her job started right now. Getting and keeping her grades up, not that she already hadn't been working on that. But thinking of horse training was much more fun than reading this book, or writing a term paper, or worst of all, algebra.

An algebra quiz on Monday morning was becoming a weekly event. DJ and all the rest of the class groaned when the teacher began handing out papers.

"But we had one last week," one of the boys said.

"And there'll probably be one next week, too. I'll try to mix up the days if that will make you feel better. Then you can look forward to it all week." Mr. Henderson gave an evil laugh that brought only a few snickers from the class.

Please, God, help me think well. Calm me down and make me remember what I've learned. If only she had spent more time reviewing last night.

But DJ buckled right in and read through the problems very carefully. Then like Robert had told her, she picked out one that she felt certain she knew how to work and did it. Then the next. While she still had two out of the ten to do when the teacher called time, she let out a big sigh of relief. She *had* answered some of them right. She didn't think she'd flunked.

"I forgot to tell you." Bridget flagged DJ down on her way to the barn that afternoon. "Would you please prepare Patches for a showing to prospective buyers tomorrow? Groom him well, put him through his paces, and wear him down some so they can ride him."

"This person *is* an experienced rider, right?"

"That is what she said. I have already warned her that Patches can be a handful, and she sounded excited. I will not let her buy him if I do not think she can handle him."

"Good. I have a favor to ask you, too."

"Yes?"

"Would you please come to my girls' class and act as a judge tomorrow? I want to remind them what a show-ring feels like, and having someone different will make it seem more real."

"What about Andrew?"

"He can do the Walk/Jog part, and I'll keep him busy down at the end of the arena while you are judging the girls."

"Sounds like you have it all worked out. Of course I will."

DJ gave Patches a good grooming, all the while reminding him that he needed to behave the next day. She saddled him without time on the hot walker and took him out to the arena. By the time he'd jogged around the ring four or five times, spooked at two shadows, and snorted at something only he saw, he finally settled down to doing what DJ asked of him. He turned, backed, changed leads in a figure eight, changed gaits when asked, and even let DJ open and close the gate from his back.

"You do as well tomorrow and you'll make me real proud of you." DJ rubbed his ears and fed him two extra horse cookies. "I'm going to miss you, you know that?"

"Me too." Mrs. Johnson stopped outside his stall. "He's

a handful, but he is fun, too. I just wish I were a better rider. . . ."

"You're doing the right thing."

"I sure hope so. Andrew says he's glad. Guess that makes it worth it, too." She gave Patches a carrot and stroked his nose. "Bridget and I are going up to see that other horse on Friday. You think I'll get to feel the same about her if it works out that I buy her?"

"I've only owned one horse, Major, and I can't see ever letting him go. Bridget kept Megs." Megs was one of Bridget's horses from international competition.

"I feel like I'm selling a friend, and that just doesn't seem right." Patches rubbed his nose against her cast. "Yeah, you caused that, you wild one, you." Patches snorted at the smell of it and rubbed his forehead on her shoulder.

"See you later, DJ. Patches, you behave tomorrow."

"You coming over?"

"I don't think so. Well, maybe. I have to bring Andrew to his lesson. Funny, I was so mad at this critter that day he dumped me in the fence, and now that he'll be leaving, all I want to do is bawl."

DJ swallowed the lump she felt growing in her own throat at the sheen of tears in the woman's eyes. "I'll do my best with him."

"I know you will."

The next day went according to plan. By the time the prospective buyer arrived, DJ had Patches well in hand. He twitched his tail when asked to work the gate and when made to walk when he wanted to keep jogging, but otherwise he behaved.

DJ patted his neck and told him how good he was before turning him over to the slender woman who at least knew horse talk. She could tell Bridget approved of the buyer.

"I'll take him," the woman said at the end of her ride.

"Good. But you might want to talk with DJ about some of his little tricks. She knows him better than anyone." Bridget laid her hand on DJ's shoulder.

"Looks to me like you've done a good job with him," the woman said after Bridget headed back to her office.

"Thank you, but I have one major rule with Patches. Always put him on the hot walker first or else plan on plenty of time to settle him down."

"I don't have a hot walker, but I can lunge him." She stroked Patches' neck and shoulder. "He seems willing."

"Today. Tomorrow he might be a firecracker ready to explode. I've kind of learned to read him, but just always be prepared. He likes to catch you if you shift your attention."

"You really are a character, aren't you?" The buyer rubbed Patches' ears and scratched his cheek. "I think we will do just fine, and maybe this summer we'll see you at the local horse shows."

Patches nodded and blew horse cookie crumbs and fumes all over them.

"I have a surprise for you," DJ told her girls as they filed into the ring a bit later.

"What?"

"We're going up in Briones?"

"You brought chocolate chip cookies." This from Krissie, who loved chocolate like Bugs Bunny loved carrots.

"No, no. Today we're going to pretend this is the show-ring, and we're going to have a judge and everything, just like you will on Saturday."

Andrew looked at her, his eyes growing round.

"Don't worry, Andrew. You and I are gonna work down at the end of the arena. These three only get up to here." She drew a line in the dirt.

"So who's the judge?"

"I am." Bridget let herself in the gate. "And we will now begin. Circle to the right, please . . . jog."

DJ kept one eye on the girls and one on Andrew. He handled a walk well now, sitting easily in the saddle and even smiling once in a while. When she asked him to trot, he swallowed, remembered to sit up straight, and squeezed his legs. Bandit obediently picked up his feet to the faster gait without fighting the bit for more speed.

"Remember what I've said about sitting deep in the saddle, and keep your heels down, back straight, good. Easy hands. Good." DJ felt pride in her young student well up within her and nearly burst out her head. *Andrew, you are doing soooo good.* But she kept her voice even. "Okay, now walk and reverse. Easy, keep him on the rail."

When she told him to, Andrew reined Bandit into the center of the ring where DJ stood. "How do you feel?"

He looked at her, a slow grin changing his face from sober to sunshine. "I like it."

DJ wanted to throw her arms around him and hug him until he squeaked. "Me too, Andrew. Me too."

The girls rode over to join them when Bridget left the arena with a wave to DJ and Andrew.

"Oh man, DJ, did you see what she did? She made us dismount, change sides, mount again." Krissie made it sound as though they'd climbed Mount Everest.

"And we had to switch horses."

"Good practice. You might be doing that on Saturday."

"I know, but Bridget is . . ." The three girls looked at one another and rolled their eyes.

"So if you could do it for her, you can do it for any old judge. Now the butterflies won't be so bad. Just tell 'em, 'Look, butterflies, we showed under Bridget Sommersby,' and they'll fly in formation for sure."

The three left the ring giggling as usual and teasing Andrew about a little girl who followed him around like a puppy.

DJ hustled back to the barn. She still hadn't had time to work Major.

And speaking of butterflies, she had better take some of her own advice. When she thought about the upcoming show and all the shows after that, the butterflies went to her brain and made her feel light-headed. Was there such a thing as butterfly brain?

11

"DJ, A SEAN MACLAINE CALLED," Lindy said when DJ got home.

"Really?"

"Who is he?"

"One of the guys I met at the art class. He's from Palo Alto." DJ stuck her head in the fridge to find a snack.

"Don't eat anything now. Dinner will be ready in a few minutes. I told him you'd call him back later."

"Okay." DJ emerged with a handful of baby carrots. For some odd reason—in fact, she couldn't remember ever doing such before—DJ walked over, kissed her mother on the cheek, and headed for her room to clean up.

The boys met her in the middle of the stairs, pelting down as fast as she was leaping up.

"We gots to set the table."

"We saw a dog."

"Hurry, DJ."

"Huh?" She stopped at the top and looked over the railing. "What dog?"

The boys stopped their charge and looked up at her, two round faces framed by squared-off bangs. "At the pound. Her name is Queenie. She licked my face." They ran their sentences together—as usual.

"What kind of dog?"

"Black." They galloped off, giggles floating back to remind DJ they had indeed been there. She debated going after them and pumping her mother for information but decided getting cleaned up would make her more popular. A dog. They were really going to get a dog. But they hadn't said if she was a puppy. No, not with a name like Queenie. An older dog, half grown. But what kind? Were they getting her for sure or. . . ?

DJ washed and dressed in double time.

"She's about a year old. The people who owned her before discovered their little boy was allergic to dogs, so they had to get rid of her. She's part Lab and . . ." Lindy shrugged. "Kind of a mixture, I guess."

"She liked us."

"She's had all her shots and seems to have been well trained."

"How come you didn't bring her home?" Robert asked. "Sounds like she belongs here."

"Well, I . . . I thought we should all see her first."

DJ rolled her lips together to keep from laughing. Her mother was *not* a dog lover. She was the main reason they'd never had a dog. In fact, her mother wasn't much of an animal lover at all.

"Okay. DJ, can you make time tomorrow right after school? Shouldn't take us long."

"I'll make it. My lesson isn't until four."

"We gets a dog. We gets a dog."

DJ felt like joining their chant. For a change the twins were right on.

"Oh, and, DJ, I forgot, but there's mail for you. From that gift shop in Connecticut."

DJ excused herself and found the envelope on the counter in the kitchen by the phone. She opened it as she made her way back to the table. A check lay in the folds of the paper.

"She paid for the last shipment and ordered two dozen more. Wait till Amy sees this," DJ spoke as she read. She looked up at her parents. "And more of the Stormy prints, too. She says those foal cards just trot right off the display they set up on the counter." DJ sank into her chair and re-read the letter. "That shop was the trial, and now she plans to carry them in her other shop, too. She asked if Amy could do some horse pictures, too, since those go over very well." She read from the letter.

"Man, oh man. Wait until I tell Mrs. Adams."

"You better tell Amy first. And I'd suggest you call Bottomly Farms and ask if they'd like to carry the note cards. They should sell a lot of merchandise from their tack shop the day of the show. That would give you more exposure around here." Lindy handed one of the boys her napkin to help mop up the water he spilled.

"Don't worry," she said when Bobby apologized. "No big deal."

DJ blinked at her mother's calm reaction to the spill. She sure was different lately. "Good idea. You really think they'd like to carry our notes?"

"Never hurts to ask."

"If they do, that means we'll have to go back to the printer soon." DJ chewed in between talking.

"Seems to me the two of you have a good thing going," Robert said. "You better start thinking of setting it up like a real business. Get a separate bank account, that kind of thing. Maybe you should make your mother the marketing person. She could set up accounts while she is home on leave."

"Set up accounts?" DJ could feel her eyes stretch along with her mind. "You mean we might have a real business after all our crazy money schemes?"

"Looks that way to me." Robert nodded and smiled at both Lindy and DJ. "Be a real success story for that book you've been thinking about."

"The one on kids and businesses?" DJ looked at her mother. "You still thinking about that?"

Lindy nodded. "It's been bugging me lately. And now this . . ."

"Gran would say God is talking loud and clear."

"I know, she told me that already." Lindy wiped her mouth with her napkin. "If no one wants any more of the scalloped potatoes, we have dessert."

"Then can we go see Queenie?" the twin who didn't have a wet front asked.

"Not until tomorrow. The Humane Society is closed now."

"But what if someone else likes her?"

"They said they'd keep her for us to decide first."

DJ let out a sigh of relief. She already thought of Queenie as theirs, and she hadn't even seen her yet.

When she called Sean, he wasn't home. So they would have to play phone tag.

But Amy was home, and she let out a shriek that nearly broke DJ's eardrum. She held the phone away from her ear and made a face at it. "You done now?"

"You won't believe this, but I just took three whole rolls of film of some pinto babies Mom and I saw. They were so cute, and if these turn out . . . Is God awesome or what?"

Queenie took one look at DJ and glued herself to her leg. She licked one boy's face, then the other and Robert's hand, sending a tail wag and friendly glance at Lindy.

"This is one smart dog." DJ leaned down and rubbed the black ears. She had a white diamond on her chest and one white back foot. One ear stood up, giving the medium-sized dog a quizzical expression. Her tail never quit wagging.

"Looks to me like she adopted you, not the other way around," the woman at the Humane Society said with a smile. She looked at the twins. "Now, you boys make sure that she gets lots of exercise . . ."

"That won't be hard," DJ said in an aside to Robert.

". . . and that she gets fed morning and night."

"And lots of water, huh?" one of the Bs said with the other nodding, their faces serious for a change.

"That's right. It takes big boys to care for a dog."

"Uh-huh." They nodded. "We're big."

"Looks like we better run by the pet store." Robert held the door for them to leave. DJ held the leash Queenie's first family had sent with their dog. The collar said "Queenie" on a brass plate. Queenie walked beside DJ as though they'd been doing this for years. She jumped in the back of the Bronco, her head over the backseat, panting in the twins' ears.

"We'll drop you off at the Academy, okay?" Looking in the rearview mirror, Robert caught DJ's gaze.

"Sure, thanks." She kept one hand on the dog.

"Now, I want to make this clear: Queenie will be sleeping in the garage," Lindy said firmly. "We'll get her a bed and . . ."

Groans from all three in the backseat.

"Now, kids, we have to get to know her, and she must get to know us. We need to make sure she remembers that she is housebroken."

"So she won't pee on the rug?"

"Yucky."

"Boys."

The twins looked at each other and giggled.

"You guys don't need a pet. You've got each other." DJ

ruffled their hair. "Take care of Queenie, now." She looked at Robert and shook her head. "We have to give her a better name than that." And with that she stepped from the car and headed for the barn.

As she reached the door, Patches' new owner was leading him out of the barn. "You got here just in time to say good-bye." She stopped and let DJ pet him.

"You behave yourself, now, you hear?" DJ dug in her pocket. Nothing. "Just a minute."

She dashed into the tack room and grabbed a carrot out of the sack she kept there. Breaking it in pieces, she palmed one for him and rubbed his ears. "I better not get any bad reports." Patches nosed for a second treat and she gave him one. "Horse cookies are his favorite, carrots a bad second. But I think he'll eat about anything. I pulled a candy wrapper out of his mouth one day."

"Thank you for training him. Bridget said again what a good job you've done. Has he ever been ridden English?"

DJ shook her head. "Not that he wouldn't look good under it. He's stylish enough to show that way."

"I'm thinking about it. Thanks again." She led Patches off to the trailer at the end of the parking lot.

When DJ heard a sniff behind her, she turned to find Mrs. Johnson wiping her eyes.

"We are such suckers about our horses, I know." She blew her nose. "If this other horse turns out, I'll be riding again next week. I can't wait." She tucked her tissue into her pocket. "DJ, I have a favor to ask. Would you be willing to ride this new horse for me a couple of times and see how she goes, then teach me?"

"Sure, ah . . ." DJ paused. "I don't have a lot of time."

"I know. Just a couple days?"

"Did you check with Bridget?"

"Uh-huh. She said to ask you."

"Tell you what—I'll ride her one time and then we'll go from there."

"Okay. That might be enough." Mrs. Johnson started to walk away, then stopped. "And, DJ, thanks for the drawing you did of Patches. It makes me smile every time I look at it. You caught his spirit and personality so perfectly."

"Patches is quite a character."

"I thought you weren't going to take on anything else?" Amy looked after the departing woman.

"I'm not."

"You did."

"I know. What could I say?"

" 'No, thank you. I don't have time.' " Amy grinned, her braces sporting bright red and blue bands. " 'Oh, I have to ask my mommy.' "

"F-u-n-n-y!"

Bridget drilled DJ on her upcoming classes just as she'd done for the girls. Walk, trot, canter, reverse.

DJ figured she'd be hearing the commands in her sleep. Thursday they reviewed the jumping and hunter classes.

"You have to remember to relax," Bridget reminded DJ. "When you get uptight, you transfer that tension to Major. You have to put the audience and judges right out of your mind. Concentrate. Concentrate. Focus. Focus. And relax. Breathe."

"And count. I forget to count."

"You are learning. But for now, concentrate on a clean round. We will worry about speed later."

DJ patted Major's neck. "We'll do our best, huh, big fellah?"

Friday was clean tack and wash horses day at the Academy. Water fights at the wash racks, soap rag rubbings in the aisles. A visitor would have thought it was one big party with all the laughter and teasing going on.

Butterflies didn't have time to play that way.

Saturday morning when they got to Bottomly, the host ranch on Bear Valley Road, one of the young riders threw up strictly from nerves. Trucks, trailers, and motor homes lined the fences and parking area, including that of a neighboring farm. Since the show would start at 9:00, horses were already warming up in the arenas before 7:00.

DJ caught a yawn with her hand and stretched, feeling both tight and tired. Since space was at a premium, horses were tied to the trailers they came in or left inside them. She made her way around the vehicles, checking on her girls. She left them grooming their horses, checked her list against that of the women handling registration, and headed back to Joe's trailer to work with Major. They had English showing in the covered arena, Western in the one outside, and Jumping/Trail classes in the one nearest the road. Only by running three rings could they fit all the classes into one day. And still the show promised to run until dark.

The second class out, DJ waited to enter the ring. Since they were showing only Equitation, the butterflies zooming around in her middle surprised her. She took a deep breath and let it out, smiling when Major did the same. As the line began moving, she clucked Major into a trot and followed the other entries into the ring. Walk, trot around the ring, and follow the judge's signals. Stand at attention. Major relaxed as the judge walked around him, and DJ groaned inside. She twitched her reins to keep him alert.

They didn't come even close to a ribbon, although they weren't last, either.

"Well, now we got our first one out of the way. The others should be easier."

"Don't feel bad," Joe said as they walked back to the trailer. "Major is a good horse, but he's just not as pretty as some of those others out there."

"Like that black-and-white paint? Talk about showy." DJ rubbed Major's nose. "But like Gran always says, 'Beauty is only skin deep and character is what counts.'"

"He's enough of a character, that's for sure." Joe gave Major a carrot piece. "And not much we can do about the pretty part."

"Here, would you take him?" DJ handed Joe the reins. "I'll be right back." She made sure the girls were getting their clothes on and hustled back to Major.

"You're going to wear a track between here and there," Joe said, giving Ranger an extra rub with a soft cloth. "Next time I'll make sure we park side-by-side." He looked DJ in the eye. "You had anything to eat yet?"

She shook her head. "No time."

Joe pointed to the cab of the truck. "Gran made sure there was food for you. Eat. Now."

DJ did as he said and could feel her butterflies settle down. They must have been hungry, too.

"Heads up! Horse loose!"

DJ looked up in time to see the black-and-white paint charge by, lead shank flapping in the breeze. So much for pretty. He probably didn't have a brain to go along with the good looks. DJ stroked Major's neck and leaned against him. "You have more common sense in one ear than that horse does in his entire body." Major nodded in agreement.

In Hunter Seat she was excused early. They gave six ribbons, and the class had numbered about twenty. The man on the paint placed sixth. That irked DJ more than anything else, other than her own early exit.

"So what did we do wrong?" she asked Bridget.

"You did not do anything wrong. The others just did things better." Bridget looked up from her clipboard to the novice English Equitation class entering the ring. "You were up against some tough competition in that class. You watch. It will be different in the Amateur Open over Fences."

All three of her girls got ribbons, much to their delight, and Angie even placed in Trail-Riding. Krissie's horse took one look at the bridge and backed clear across the arena. However, when it was time to back up on command, he refused.

Amy took second in Western Equitation and first in Trail. "I think I'm going to start working with poles and barrels," she said as she and DJ sat watching Joe, who was waiting for his turn in the senior Western Pleasure class.

"Good idea. Josh will be good at that. He's quick on his feet and smart as all get out."

Up behind them in the bleachers, the entire family had gathered to root for DJ and Joe.

"When's Grandpa's turn?"

"Pretty soon," Lindy answered.

But in spite of their cheering, Ranger missed a couple of signals and didn't place.

"No ribbon?" Bobby and Billy both looked ready to go out in the ring and take on the judge.

"Maybe next time. This was Grandpa's first time competing. He did pretty good."

"No ribbon." The plaintive sound of the boy's voice made DJ grin and Amy giggle.

They knew just how Joe was feeling right then. Crummy.

"I think they should give him a ribbon just for trying, an old man like that."

"Robert John Crowder, what a thing to say about your

father." Lindy smacked him on the arm. "I'm going to tell him you said that, too."

Robert used his program to tap DJ on the head. "One more class and it's your turn."

"Thanks for reminding me. Come on, Ames, you can help us get ready."

"Thanks a *whole* lot." The two levered themselves off the bleachers and headed back to the trailer.

DJ's butterflies took the opportunity to go wild.

12

"GOOD LUCK," TONY ANDRADA SAID, touching his whip to his helmet.

"You too." DJ sent him a smile that was supposed to be encouraging. Instead, it felt like it cracked her face. *You know better than to let this get to you. Come on, relax and go with the flow.*

"Easy for you to say." While she mumbled mostly to herself, Joe turned to look at her.

"What's up?" He grinned and shook his head. "Not what's up, but what's down, huh?"

DJ nodded. "I want to do good so b-a-d."

"All anyone can ask is that you do your best."

"Yeah, and you can't do your best when you're tighter than a drum. I better walk him around."

"He's not the one that's uptight." Joe tapped her knee as she turned Major away. Once more around the warm-up ring might help.

Father in heaven, all I ask is that you help me do my best. She wanted to say "and win," but she decided not to. Tony trotted beside her.

"You okay?"

"I will be."

"Yeah, me too. The waiting is a killer." He paused to listen to the number of the contestant entering the ring. "I'm next."

DJ rode beside him back to the gate. She wanted to watch him and cheer him on. That's what the Academy kids did for one another.

She heard a sharp crack and knew a rail had gone down. A brief spatter of applause and the gatekeeper swung the gate open to let the other rider out.

DJ could see Tony take a deep breath and let his shoulders relax. She caught herself doing the same thing. He nudged his horse forward and trotted into the ring.

"He is one cool-looking dude," a young girl off to the side said to another.

DJ glanced at her grandfather and, by the grin on his face, knew he had heard, too.

Tony took the first fence with what looked like three feet to spare, but by the second he had settled down to business.

DJ could feel herself counting with him. She leaned forward at the same time he did.

Major shifted and pricked his ears. Tension hummed through his body. He was as ready as she.

Tony and his horse jumped a clean round. The third one of the class.

"Go get 'em, tiger," Tony called as he rode by. "And have fun."

DJ smiled up at her family and squeezed her legs. "This is it, big boy. Let's go."

Major took the first jump with room to spare, as if he were saying, "Let's get me something to jump." He kept his ears forward and snorted when they landed after the oxer. The stone wall made him twitch his tail as he looked forward to the triple.

Each time he lifted off, DJ felt as though they were flying, sailing free like the birds in the air. Major landed so perfectly, always looking to the next jump, always responding to her signals. Together they jumped clean and received a round of hearty applause. Of course, it helped that half the grandstand was either related to her or rode for Briones.

She wanted to hug the entire world and half the universe. "We did it! Joe, we did it. A clean round. I can't tell you how much fun that was."

"I think you just did. And the light in this old boy's eyes says the same thing. You are two of a kind. Adrenaline junkies, for sure."

Major rubbed his forehead against Joe's shoulder, nearly knocking him over.

"All right, so you're not junkies."

The next rider ticked and the bar wobbled enough that it finally fell. The audience groaned.

By the end of the twelve jumpers, four had jumped a perfect round. DJ was the youngest.

She, Tony, and others waited while the ring officials raised the jumps. Major snorted as she walked him in a circle to keep him loosened up.

"I know, you're just a-rarin' to go back out there." She patted his neck and swapped proud looks with Joe.

One of the other girls jumped first and knocked a rail down. The second jumped a clean round. Tony did the same.

And so did DJ.

The crowd went wild. DJ could hear the twins screaming her name. Was that her mother's voice she heard, too? She didn't dare look.

Bridget leaned on the wooden fencing off to the side of the practice ring. "You have done well, ma petite. Just continue as you are, relaxed and having a good time. Major is just eating this up."

The girl ticked one and sent another rail rocking to the

ground. The crowd sighed with her and gave her a rousing hand as she cantered out of the arena.

Tony jumped clean.

Father, help me. The center rail on the triple was higher than she had ever jumped.

"Okay, kid, here's where they separate the men from the boys, er, the . . ." Joe shrugged and grinned up at her. "You just do your best, Darla Jean Randall."

DJ trotted into the ring.

The jumps looked six feet high. How could a few inches make such a difference?

She signaled Major into a canter and headed for the first jump, a post and rail. When they cleared it, she swallowed and aimed Major for the next. Ears forward, he lifted into the air at just the right time and cleared the jump as though he was out to play.

The wall, the oxer. DJ leaned into them, lifting him over with her hands and legs. The final jump loomed before them. "Easy now." They left the ground—and at that instant she knew.

His hind foot ticked the bar.

They had won second place.

"I'm sorry, fellah. That was my fault." She patted his neck and bit back the crud in her throat. Crying was for losers and sissies, and they were neither. She smiled for the judge and the camera, congratulated Tony, and rode out of the ring.

"I got left behind," she whispered to Joe. "It was my fault, not that he couldn't clear that thing."

"Sorry, DJ, but second place and going three rounds is nothing to sneeze at." Joe smoothed Major's neck and whispered in his ear, "I am so proud of you, old man, that I could pop."

"We could have gotten the blue."

"Yes, you could have. Or another round and you might

have gotten the same thing." Bridget gave DJ her no-nonsense look.

"I got left behind."

"I know. So next time, you will not to do it again. The two of you cleared jumps higher than you have ever jumped before. Now, be pleased with that accomplishment and do not"—her stern face lent credence to her words—"cut yourself down."

Tony walked his horse up to her. "DJ Randall, you did awesome. I happen to know for a fact that is only the second time you two have entered a jumping competition. You and Major have really come a long way."

"Thank you. You two were supremo. Were you having as much fun as it looked?"

He nodded, eyes sparkling. "We sure were." He patted his horse's sweaty neck. "We sure were."

"Good going," Hilary called from the practice arena.

"Good luck," Tony and DJ called at the same time. Hilary would be competing in the open Jumping class since she was older than eighteen.

"You want me to put him away so you can watch Hilary?" Joe asked.

"Thanks, GJ." DJ swung her leg over and slid to the ground. She gave Major one last pat and joined her family and Amy up in the stands. The boys oohed and ahhed over her ribbon, and Robert gave her a pat on the back. Lindy made an okay sign with her thumb and index finger.

Hilary was the second to jump and the first to make a clean round. Three tries later and she took the top ribbon out of the ring with her, Bunny placing second. For the second time that day, first and second in a jumping class were taken by riders from Briones.

"That is a young woman to watch," DJ heard someone say from up in the stands. "She's going for the big time, mark my words."

134

"You said the same about the young blonde in the class before."

"I know, and have you ever known me to be wrong?"

When DJ glanced over at Amy, she knew they'd both heard the same thing.

"Sure hope he's right this time," Amy whispered. "I get to go along as your groom."

"Yeah, right." DJ rolled her eyes as she poked Amy with her elbow.

"DJ, can I ride Major?"

"Me too?"

DJ rose and took a boy's hand in each of hers. "Sure, come on. Major would love some company right about now."

"Are you staying for the rest of the show?" Robert asked.

"No, we'll leave as soon as we get packed up. I'll take these guys over to Joe first."

"Good, tell him I'll be over to get them in a few minutes."

"You want to pack note cards tomorrow after church?" Amy asked after they put their horses back in their own stalls and closed up the barn. "You know Bottomly sold all we brought them."

"I guess. Mom has some stuff she says she wants to talk over with us."

"Darla Jean Randall, let it go!" Amy socked her friend in the arm.

"What?"

"Oh, come off it. You think I can't read you like a book? So you made a mistake. It wasn't the first time, and you can bet it won't be the last. If Bridget saw your sad face, she'd be livid."

DJ sucked in a big breath and let it all out. "Sorry. I'm trying not to think about it."

"Well, don't just try. Do it!"

"Easy for you to say. You're not the one who—" DJ stopped at the look on her friend's face. Amy was right. She for sure didn't want Bridget on her case.

"Controlling one's thoughts is just as important as controlling one's body." DJ could hear Bridget. If she'd heard those words once, she'd heard them a gazillion times.

Now to put them into practice.

The next afternoon after church, Lindy gave them a short course in business management while they packaged the remaining note cards and boxed them for shipping. Both girls groaned when they heard the words *checking account*.

"What's wrong with the way we do things now?" Amy asked.

"What do you do?"

"Split everything right down the middle."

"Both expenses and reimbursements?"

"Right. If that's what you call the money."

"So what happens if one product really takes off and sells lots more than any of the rest?"

"Uh . . ." DJ and Amy shrugged.

"If anything takes off and sells like crazy, it'll be way cool." Amy taped the last packet of note cards closed. "I took two of the new photos down to the printer. Those cards will be ready next week."

DJ glanced at her watch. Time was fleeing and she needed to be studying. Robert had said he'd help her review her algebra later. But this time with her mother was important, too; any idiot could tell that. Always so many decisions to make, and not easy ones, either.

"So I think you need tracking numbers on each packet, and you need to make up a catalog to show to new markets."

"John's a computer genius. He could do that for us." DJ looked to Amy for confirmation.

"Yeah, and I'll probably have to do his chores for life to pay him back."

The discussion continued until Amy had to go home—with nothing decided and lots more for DJ to think about.

And there were midterms this week.

13

"YOU CAN ALWAYS SHOW BOTH Major and Herndon," Jackie said over the phone Monday evening.

"Right now I can't keep up with one. This is midterms week, and I'm trying to get ready for the show next weekend."

"What do you have to get ready?"

"Bridget is drilling me on the flat and over the fences." DJ twisted the phone cord around her finger. "We're repainting tack boxes at the barn, so our stalls will look really good. One of the mothers even sewed new canvas for the folding chairs." She propped her feet up on her desk and leaned back in her chair. "Bridget designed a new sign, too." Having a phone of her own did have some advantages. But at the same time, she thought with longing of her old room. Granted, it was smaller and she'd had to share a bathroom with the twins. But no matter, it was home and this was ... She wondered sometimes if she wasn't living in nowhere land. She wasn't a guest here— although guests didn't have to clear the table and do dishes—but she wasn't home, either.

She felt more at home at Jackie and Brad's than she did here.

Queenie whined from the place she'd adopted beside DJ's desk.

"I better go and get back to studying. Oh—one other thing. Bridget thinks I should stick with Hunter classes at this show, so I guess I will. Thanks for the offer. I'll see you at the show on Saturday, right?"

"Right. Sorry we couldn't come last week."

Me too, DJ thought as she hung up the phone. *If I didn't win there, there's no chance I'm gonna win anything at a big show. They'll probably take one look at us and point down the road.*

Knowing this was the next step and having any confidence at all were two very different things.

A knock at the door brought Queenie's ears up and DJ's feet to the floor. "You ready for a math review?" Robert asked.

"Sure." She dug her algebra book out of the stack. "Come on in." When he stuck his head in the door, she asked, "Here or down there?"

"The fireplace is going, Mom's popping corn, and the boys are about to hit the sack."

"Down there, then."

"I think she's your dog." Robert nodded to the shadow glued to DJ's knee.

"I know. Funniest thing. I haven't done anything to make her think that."

"She adopted you right from the moment she saw you. But according to the lady at the Humane Society, the family had only one child, the boy with allergies."

"Funny, huh?" They descended the stairs, three abreast.

"Furniture's supposed to come tomorrow." He nodded to the empty living room. "I'll be glad when the house is all put together. Maybe pretty soon we can get started on the barn. Have you been thinking about stabling Major here and riding over to the Academy?"

"Not really. Is that what you want me to do?"

"It's up to you."

Robert had used that phrase with her more than once. More decisions to make. They spent about an hour reviewing algebra, and at the end of it, Robert smiled, shaking his head.

"I am amazed. DJ, I think you've got it. What has made the difference?"

DJ wrinkled her forehead so she could think better. She squinted her eyes and rolled her lips together. "I . . . I'm not sure. Maybe it all came together. You guys all convinced me I could do it, and I got the nerve to ask my teacher to explain things again and really listened. No more zoning out." She paused. "I've really been praying, and I know others have, too. And," she paused, deepening her voice for effect, "I got a B on my last quiz."

"Good for you." He patted her on the knee. "What tests are tomorrow?"

"Besides algebra? PE, but that's just on basketball skills. No sweat."

"You two want hot fudge sundaes?" Lindy broke into their discussion.

"Sure." DJ slapped the book closed.

"So how'd you do?" Amy asked when they met back at their lockers the next morning.

"No clue. At least I understood the questions. I ran out of time." DJ leaned her head against the cold locker door. "Makes me feel so stupid."

"DJ!"

"Well, I gave it my best shot." She tipped her head to the side and shrugged. "Now I just have to finish my term paper by Friday and throw up every time I think of the show on Saturday. You ready for lunch?"

She had no test in art but needed to finish the project she was working on, another still life, this one of an old boot lying on its side, an empty gold leaf picture frame, and a lone pink tulip in a bud vase. Her training from Isabella Gant in San Francisco regarding negative space made the still life come together. She chose to do the entire picture in black pencil, then tinted the tulip a soft pink and touched a few places on the frame with gold metallic.

"That's an interesting rendering." Mrs. Adams stood right behind DJ, looking over her shoulder. "What if you deepened the shading on the top of that boot? Might give it more definition. Don't be afraid of contrasts." She nodded again when DJ looked up at her. "I like it."

DJ turned back to her picture. She liked it, too. "You want to see my latest foal picture?"

"Sure enough."

This time Stormy stood with her front feet far apart, sniffing a dandelion.

"Oh, DJ, what a charmer." She picked up the drawing pad and held it so the light was better. "Are you going to put this in your card line?"

"Um-hmm." DJ narrowed her eyes at her still life and added darker lines on the boot top, erasing other places to lighten them. That *was* better. What her teacher had said sank in. "Card line?"

"Why, yes, I see you coming up with an entire line of foal pictures. Cards, prints, T-shirts. You wait and see."

"You're putting me on, right?"

"No." Mrs. Adams shook her head. "Not at all."

Immediately a picture of Stormy looking up at a butterfly came to DJ's mind. Her fingers itched to get started.

Mrs. Adams set the pad down and studied the still life again. "Good." She moved on to the next student.

Wish all my classes were like this one. When the bell

rang, DJ slung her pack over her shoulder and followed the others out the door. What would it be like to go to art school like Mrs. Adams had suggested once? Would it be possible to do that and prepare for the Olympics at the same time? Ms. Gant had even mentioned once a high school in San Francisco for kids who wanted to spend their time with art.

DJ brought her attention back to Acalanese High School. Here she'd started and here she'd finish. No way could she take the time to commute to San Francisco. Next fall she'd be in a pottery class. Now, that would be something different.

By Friday night she felt wrung out from lack of sleep as she finished her term paper and the last book report, plus all the other studying. Thinking about the morning only made her feel like hiding under the covers and not coming out.

"DJ, are you feeling all right?" her mother asked.

"Ask me on Sunday." DJ rubbed her forehead. "Do you mind if I just eat a sandwich and go to bed?"

"We're having lasagna."

"I don't think I could even eat it." Getting Major ready for transporting and then showing in the morning had taken the last bit of energy she had. She should have been helping decorate the stalls and setting up at the show. But her tests had come first. Joe had helped Bunny and Bridget. "Can you save me some?"

"Sure enough. Peanut butter and jam all right?"

"And a piece of cheese." DJ slumped on the stool.

"You sick, DJ?" The boys looked up at her, eyes serious for a change.

She shook her head. "Just beat."

Queenie yipped at the back door, and one boy ran to let her in. She made a beeline for DJ and put her two front paws up on DJ's leg.

"Down, girl." Queenie dropped to all fours, her head cocked and a doggy grin showing her pink tongue.

DJ ruffled her ears and got a nose lick for her trouble.

The boys giggled and DJ couldn't help but smile. The boys knelt on either side of the dog and laid their heads on her back. Queenie gave each of them a lightning lick and wriggled all over.

"She sure has made herself at home here." DJ picked up the cheese from the plate her mother set in front of her.

"What do you want to drink?"

"Milk. I need all the energy I can get." DJ stared at her food. "I think my eyes are crossing."

Bobby—DJ could tell because he had a scrape on his chin—peered up at her. "No, your eyes are straight."

"That's a figure of speech to say she's tired." Lindy gave each boy a baby carrot and put a couple on DJ's plate.

DJ picked up her plate and glass. "Thanks, Mom. You have no idea how much I appreciate this. See you tomorrow evening."

The boys and Queenie followed her upstairs, as if making sure she could get there. Billy even folded back her bedspread and blanket.

"Night, DJ. Sleep tight and don't let the bed bugs bite."

The two looked at each other and giggled. "Bed bugs, eeuwie!"

"I won't." She ushered them out of the room and closed her door. She drained the milk, taking bites of her sandwich while she undressed. She'd finished the cheese on the way up the stairs.

She didn't even remember pulling up the blankets.

Joe pulled into the drive at 5:45 A.M., and DJ was still sound asleep, her alarm buzzing like it had been for the last half hour.

"DJ, Dad's here. How long until you'll be ready?"

"Oh my goodness." She threw back the covers and her feet hit the floor running. "Ten minutes."

"Take your time, DJ. I'll go load Major and come back for you." Joe had joined Robert at her bedroom door.

"Or I can bring her over," Robert offered.

"I'm almost ready." At least she'd packed her things the morning before. She grabbed the clothes bag with her showing clothes and threw open her door. "Here, would you please carry this down? I'll get the rest." It was hard to talk around the scrunchie clamped in her teeth.

DJ ate her breakfast in the truck and curled up for a nap after that. The others had gone over the night before, so they were alone. Joe woke her in time for her to redo her hair and begin to look like she understood this was morning—show morning.

While DJ had been to this arena as a spectator, this was her first time to show there. What a difference it made. The Farthingale Equestrian Center looked like a miniature fairgrounds with three show-rings: two outside and one in, plus a practice ring. Tall white painted buildings housed an exhibit area for horse- and showing-related products, food stalls, and a fenced-in play area for little kids. There were enough trailers, RVs, and fancy horse rigs to start a sale.

"One day soon, we're investing in something like that." Joe pointed to a motor home with an awning set up and folding chairs around a table. It looked more like a home than a horse-showing rig. "Especially if you're going to be showing like Bridget said."

"But they're so expensive." DJ still had trouble accepting the idea of not having to cut her dimes in half to make them go further. Life sure could be different when money wasn't such an issue.

"You let the adults worry about that part. You just give it all you've got."

And don't get the big head, her little voice snickered in her ear.

"You go on in. I'll park this and unload Major."

DJ sent him a "thank you" over her shoulder as she bailed out of the truck. Just the smell of the horse show set her nerves to humming. She followed his directions to the aisle they were assigned.

"Man, this is awesome." DJ studied the display and shook her head. "Really beautiful." The maroon banner with the Briones Acadamy logo hung on a shiny gold bar sticking out from the wall above the door to the tack room. Gold-toned name plates on each stall shone from recent polishing. Even the hay slings matched the water tubs.

"You like it?" Bunny asked, hands on hips, studying the picture and comparing it to those around them. "I think we look pretty good."

"Hi, DJ," Hilary called from inside her stall, where she was putting a final polish on her horse. You got the end stall, and it's all ready for you. Hear you're going Hunter."

DJ stopped in front of Hilary's stall. "Bridget thought that was best since this is my first rated show. That and Major doesn't seem quite up to tip-top yet. I could tell after jumping him last weekend."

Hilary nodded and smoothed down her horse's face with a soft cloth. "There's some pretty good-looking competition here. If you need any help, just ask."

"Thanks." DJ headed for the unloading area.

Ears nearly touching at the tips, Major watched everything around them as she led him into his stall. He snuffled her shoulder, then nosed the hay rack and checked out the water bucket. The horse on the other side of him banged the stall wall and laid back his ears.

Uh-oh, got a nasty one here. DJ patted Major's nose and left the stall to get her grooming bucket.

"Watch out for the snots in the next stalls," Bunny whispered as DJ opened the tack box. "They really think they're something."

The butterflies in DJ's middle took a practice flutter.

Another squeal from the stall next to them grabbed her attention. The other horse, ears flat against his head and teeth bared, lunged at the bars between him and Major.

14

IF ENTERING THE PRACTICE RING sent her butterflies cartwheeling, what would the real one do?

DJ warmed Major up carefully, not taking any chances of him pulling a tendon or something. Walking and then slow trotting around the ring gave them both a chance to look at some of the other entries. As Joe had said, there were some classy horses here.

She patted Major's shoulder, not wanting him to feel bad but knowing she was the one comparing, not him. She glanced up to see Brad and Jackie at the rail, smiles on their faces, waiting for her to see them.

They trotted over, and Brad stroked Major's nose while he greeted her.

"You two are looking good. He's moving easy."

Jackie cocked her head. "Forgive him. He's got father flutters." She grinned up at DJ.

"Father flutters?"

"You know how you felt when your students were showing and you were wringing your hands?" Brad made a worried face for her. DJ nodded. "Well, multiply it by a hundred. That's how I feel."

"I'd rather show myself any day than watch someone I love in the ring." Jackie nodded and slipped her hand through the bend at Brad's elbow. "I've got to keep him on the ground here."

DJ smiled and then giggled. Her father did indeed look—well, running his fingers through his hair had disturbed the way it usually lay, and his fingers drummed on the fence rail. "If I could, I'd give you all my butterflies to go with yours."

"Thanks a heap, kid." He smiled up at her. "You need anything? Can I get you something to eat, drink?"

"He wants an excuse to get a cup of coffee." Jackie winked at DJ. "We'll be back."

"I'll take a doughnut," DJ said and turned Major back into the ring.

Waiting in line to enter the ring for the first time took three hours. At least, it felt like three hours by the time the gatekeeper signaled DJ's turn. Junior Hunter Seat Equitation sounded easy, but when she looked at the horses ahead of them, her butterflies created new aerial maneuvers.

Walk, trot, canter, reverse. Major took it all like a pro, and DJ settled down after the first circuit of the ring. But with twenty entrants, they didn't place.

Not that she'd expected to. But DJ still felt a bit of a letdown. Winning a ribbon, even last place, felt good.

"That's okay, Deej. You two did a good job out there. You were just out-classed. Pretty counts here, you know." Brad's attempts to comfort her made her feel worse.

Maybe we shouldn't even be here. DJ banished that thought as soon as it cropped up.

Even having her own motel room didn't keep DJ awake that night. She and Joe left the others sleeping when they headed back to the barn in the early morning to care for Major.

By the next afternoon, DJ had endured three classes, all without ribbons. At her fourth and final class, DJ stiffened her spine, then ordered herself to relax. This time they had fences to take. She patted Major's neck and smiled at the gatekeeper as they waited for his signal.

Please, Lord. The prayer went no further. The signal came, and she nudged Major into a trot and entered the ring.

"Shame she doesn't have a better horse." The comment came from someone along the gate. DJ started to turn her head, but Bridget's drilling came to her rescue. *Focus. Focus. Only think of your horse and the jumps*.

Major slowed. DJ stared straight between his ears at the single post and rail in front of them. "Easy, fella, here we go." With that they sailed over the jump with air to spare. And again at the brush box with greenery growing out the top, then the in and out. The chicken coop was last. It looked like a pup tent made of plywood painted in red-and-white stripes.

DJ leaned forward. *Too soon.* Major stopped. DJ didn't. She ended up on his neck, her helmet over one eye. Major flicked his ears and popped over the fence.

DJ wished the ring floor would open and they could fall in. Instead, she found her stirrup again, gathered the reins, and as she signaled a canter again, pushed her helmet back in place. If only they could ride out of the ring and keep going until she found water to bathe her flaming face.

The refusal was all her fault. She'd hurried.

"Sorry, Major." But what could she say? She caught a glimpse of Bridget's raised eyebrow as they left the ring. Since they'd legally completed the jump, they were still in the running. Only DJ's pride had been bruised. Major took the second round without a pause, the way he would have if she hadn't messed up.

Back at the barn, as DJ put Major away, the horse next

to them reached around from his stall door and tried to bite Major again.

"Can't you make your horse behave?" DJ felt like hitting the beast with a two-by-four.

"Get over it." The girl stood talking with her teammate, and her upper lip curled.

The snobby answer made DJ clamp her teeth and clench her fist. *What a brat!* She led Major into the stall and began removing his saddle.

"Ugly old plug like that doesn't belong here anyway."

DJ knew they meant for her to hear it.

"Ignore them," Tony Andrada said from her stall door. "People with attitudes like theirs are losers." He raised his voice more than just for DJ.

DJ nodded. Bunny had warned her that people at rated shows acted differently than those at local and schooling shows did. But still . . .

She could hear Gran even over the pounding of her heart. *"Pray for those who do you wrong."* Pray for those snobs? Not on her life.

"That's okay, Major, beauty is only skin deep. And if I had a mean horse like that, I'd shoot it." She whispered the words into his ear, making him shake his head and lean his forehead against her shoulder.

DJ came from putting Major away after their final event in time to watch the jump-off for Junior Hunter. Bridget and Amy sat with her family, halfway up in the stands.

"No pretty ribbons, huh, DJ?" Bobby said softly.

"Poor DJ." Billy shook his head, a sad face getting sadder.

"Nope, not one." She tried to say it as though it didn't matter, but they all knew her too well.

"You did your best." Amy scooted over to make a place for her.

"Yup, and my best wasn't good enough."

"Yet." Bridget leaned her elbows on her knees, concentrating on the rider in the ring.

Nothing. Even at my very first horse show, I brought back one ribbon. "I musta let the butterflies get to me. Those jumps weren't hard. I just—" Catching a look from Bridget, DJ shut her mouth. *I knew better than to let what that guy said bother me.*

She felt a hand on her shoulder and turned to give Brad as much of a smile as she could muster.

"So you had a bad day. That means you got over that, through your first rated show, and now you'll be able to go forward."

Jackie took the seat in front of DJ. "At least you didn't fall off." She said that just after the rider in the ring took a nose dive to the collective gasps of the audience.

"Pretty close." But she didn't say more, knowing that Bridget would turn and give her a *look*.

"I can remember the time my horse took off on me in the ring. I thought I would die of embarrassment."

"You should have seen her face. She was so mad, she was steaming. Lobster red, she was," Brad said with a chuckle.

Another rider entered the ring. Bridget had already identified him as one of the better riders in the area.

"Watch his hands," Bridget said.

DJ concentrated on his hands and . . . "He's behind." The horse ticked a rail that wobbled and stayed in place.

The flashy bay ran out at the next jump.

He finished the circuit, but the pair exited the ring with no chance of a ribbon.

"Now, what did you learn?" Bridget turned to DJ.

"He was having a bad day?"

"Could be. What else?"

"He made some mistakes. He dropped him and the horse ran out."

"It happens to all of us, DJ. You have a choice. Keep beating on yourself, or let it go and put what you learned to work for the next show."

"Amen to that," Jackie added.

"That Bridget has a good head on her shoulders," Joe said on the way home.

"Umm."

"You're not very talkative."

DJ knew she had to throw it off. "I feel like I let Major down."

"Okay. That's a feeling, and you're entitled to your feelings. But that doesn't mean that's the whole truth."

"I know. But I hate messing up."

"Don't we all?"

The silence stretched again.

"Those girls in the stalls next to us were meaner than—"

"I know. I saw what was happening."

"As if they were perfect. They've got perfect horses and—"

Joe cut her off. "You'll meet those kind of people everywhere. Just have to learn to not let them bother you."

"I wanted to *bother* them, all right, with a two-by-four."

Joe chuckled. "Now, *that* would have made your grandmother proud."

"Wish she could have come today."

"Me too, but she couldn't leave that painting. They wanted it a week ago."

"I know." But still she missed Gran. It seemed like they never got time together anymore.

A few miles passed before Joe asked, "Did you hear the good news?"

DJ roused herself from a half sleep. "What?"

"Andy's buying your old house."

"Really?"

"Shawna wanted to come today, but they're getting their house ready for sale."

"Good."

But the heavy feeling hung on, no matter how DJ tried to talk herself out of it. If only she could go back, go home again. Yes, she wanted to jump in the Olympics, and yes, she would keep going, but . . .

The *but* stopped her.

"Are you moping?" Lindy asked on Tuesday night. "Feeling sorry for yourself?"

"I don't think so," DJ said, turning from studying the green of the hills as they drove. "It's like I've got to work this thing out in my head."

"Well, you let me know if I can help."

"Okay." She wasn't sure she had done her best; that was part of it. And the feeling of rushing, like she'd rushed that jump. And wanting to go back. Life in her old house seemed easier in her memory. She had even pulled out her old bedspread, but it didn't look right on the new bed.

When they handed out midterm reports on Thursday, she was afraid to look at hers. She couldn't go back on restrictions. Her mother wouldn't do that, would she? After DJ had been trying and trying so hard?

"So what'd you get?"

"Haven't looked."

"Darla Jean Randall, what am I going to do with you? Give me your report card." Amy held out her hand.

DJ dug it out of the front pocket of her pack and handed the envelope over.

Amy looked at it, shrugged, and handed it back. "Guess that B minus in algebra will keep your mom happy."

DJ snatched the report back and read down the line. Four As, one A minus, and the B minus in algebra. She felt like running across the parking lot screaming and dancing. "Guess it will." The two swapped high fives.

Since no one was home when she got there, she changed and rode her bike over to the Academy. The new way was much shorter than the other, but she missed the time she and Amy used to have together.

After her workout, for some reason she turned right and headed back the way to the old house. Amy's mother had picked her up, so they couldn't even ride together.

The grass had been mowed at their house. And a new coat of paint brightened the outside. She put her key in the lock and opened the door. The house smelled empty. She crossed the family room and looked out at the backyard. The gardeners had been there, too. A row of red tulips nodded in the twilight.

She turned and headed up the stairs to her old room. Halfway up she stopped and backed down to look where Gran's wing chair used to sit. She could close her eyes and feel herself sitting on the floor at Gran's knee. Gran would stroke her hair and share a Bible verse with her.

DJ sucked in a deep breath. Now Gran lived with Joe. Would she give up Joe to go back?

"No way!" She shook her head and continued up to her old room. It was so small. Well, not really, but compared to her new one it was. She sat down on the floor, back against the wall where her desk used to sit. Arms on her knees, she waited. For what, she wasn't sure.

But it remained an empty room. Not her old room, but an empty room in an empty house.

Something she'd heard once, *"You can't go back,"* now made sense.

It wasn't the same. The house wasn't it at all. It was just a house now, not her home. It would be a good home for her cousin Shawna. She'd like this room.

DJ stood and jogged back down the stairs. She locked the door behind her and pedaled back up the hill and down past the Academy, around the bend, and into the driveway. Putting her bike away in the garage, she hummed a tune under her breath as she entered the back door.

"Where've you been?" Lindy looked up from breaking lettuce into a bowl for salad.

"To our old house." DJ snagged a carrot from the plastic sack on the counter.

Lindy kept her eyes on her daughter and her hands busy with the salad.

DJ waved the carrot in the air. "You know what?"

"What?"

"You can't go back."

"So?"

"So it isn't the house."

"I don't understand. What isn't the house?"

"Well, it isn't the house that makes a home. We've moved on up to a bigger house, and while I thought it didn't feel like home, it does. I've moved up to bigger shows, and they'll feel like home eventually. I've moved up in my art, too."

She dug her midterm report out of her back pocket and tossed it on the counter.

Lindy wiped her hands on her apron and, still watching DJ, pulled the card from the envelope.

DJ kept her face as blank as she could, watching her

mother. After all, a girl who went from a D minus to a B minus in algebra in one quarter could do about anything she set her mind to. She could keep on moving up, as far as she wanted to go.

"You did it! I knew you could." Lindy threw her arms around her daughter and danced her around the kitchen.

"Me too—now."

Acknowledgments

Thanks to Joanie Jagoda, who brainstorms, coaches, and critiques not only my horse information, where she is a master, but throughout my books.

Thanks, Tim Mitchell, for your help in the field of algebra, where I, like DJ, struggle or don't as the case may be. No telling who you might sit next to on an airplane.

Thanks to Rochelle and Natasha for helping keep my timelines straight and all the other things that editors do to help books become the best they can be.

Early Teen Fiction Series From
Bethany House Publishers
(Ages 11–14)

∝∝

HIGH HURDLES • by Lauraine Snelling
Show jumper DJ Randall strives to defy the odds and achieve her dream of winning Olympic Gold.

HOLLY'S HEART • by Beverly Lewis
About to turn thirteen, Holly Meredith relies on her faith to help her through the challenges of family, school, friendships, and boys.

JANETTE OKE CLASSICS FOR GIRLS • by Janette Oke
Turn-of-the-century stories capture readers' hearts as they get to know teen girls facing the timeless challenges of growing up into Christlike young women.

SUMMERHILL SECRETS • by Beverly Lewis
Fun-loving Merry Hanson encounters mystery and excitement in Pennsylvania's Amish country.